Malcolm Macdonald

Guatemozin

A drama

Malcolm Macdonald

Guatemozin
A drama

ISBN/EAN: 9783337334260

Printed in Europe, USA, Canada, Australia, Japan

Cover: Foto ©Andreas Hilbeck / pixelio.de

More available books at **www.hansebooks.com**

A DRAMA.

BY

MALCOLM MACDONALD.

PHILADELPHIA:

J. B. LIPPINCOTT & CO.

1878.

DRAMATIS PERSONÆ.

GUATEMOZIN, King of Mexico.

THE LORD OF TACUBA.

TIZOC, a Prince of Mexico.

OYOT,
CULQUIL, } Aztec Nobles.
MAXTLA,

TUNAL, a Slave.

TECUICHPO, Queen of Mexico.

AÇALAN, Princess of Tezcuco.

A Crazy Woman.

HERNANDO CORTÉS.

ALDERETE, Royal Treasurer.

FARFAN,
PANFILIO, } Officers under Cortés.
RAMON,

ANTONIO DE VILLAFANA,
MUÑOZ,
JERONIMO,
FERNAN, } Soldiers.
PEDRO,
BAMBA,

ISTRISUCHIL, King of Tezcuco, brother of Coanaco, the deposed
   king, and usurping the throne by the countenance of Cortés.

Ambassadors, Alguazils, Conspirators; Aztec, Spanish, and Tezcucan Soldiers; Messengers and Attendants.

3

GUATEMOZIN.

GUATEMOZIN.

ACT I.

SCENE I.—MEXICO.

In the garden of the King's Palace.

[PRINCESS AÇALAN *is sitting in a bower.*]

Enter the LORD OF TACUBA.

TACUBA.

How blue the sky! What ecstasy of air!
The soothing wind touches, as gently fall
The petals of a rose on waters smooth,
Dimpling to quiver and be still again.
O how this flower is sweetening the day!
Yon bird, with melody achoke and strangling
With harmony, if throbbing throat could break,
What flood of song would inundate the air!
I seek a fairer flower, a sweeter voice.
She should be waiting here beside this agave,
That burst in bloom the day we vowed our loves.

Seeing AÇALAN, *and advancing.*

7

I will go stealthily as an ocelot,
And take her by surprise.

Pausing.

But hark ! she sings.
Hold all your breaths, and mingle not, ye winds,
With hers a baser air ; be dumb, ye birds !

AÇALAN, *singing.*

I knew a queenly rose,
 She loved the kingly sun,
And fairer grew : love beauty grows
 In every one.
Ah, love ! sweet love ! thou can'st say no,
And hearts be colder than the snow.

He wooed her all the day,
 At night his love departed.
She wept, his course she could not stay;
 Poor broken-hearted !
Ah, love ! sweet love ! thou can'st say no,
And hearts be colder than the snow.

The sun came back again,
 Alas !· he was too late.
Her drooping head revealed she then
 Was near her fate.
Ah, love ! sweet love ! thou can'st say no,
And hearts be colder than the snow.

She thrills, her bosom heaves ;
O could'st thou not abide ?
The breezes cast her pallid leaves
On every side.
Ah, love ! sweet love ! thou can'st say no,
And hearts be colder than the snow.

TACUBA *kneels by her.*

AÇALAN, *starting.*

You frighten me !

TACUBA.

O pardon—

AÇALAN.

Nay, now fear,
Since it may hide in love, shall never fright
Again.

TACUBA.

And did you sing that lover's song
Because I was 'way ?

AÇALAN.

Partly no, and yes,—
I love its melody ; I thought of you,—
You were away ; that slight suggestion call'd
The song to mind, and then its words woke thoughts

Of Tezcuco,—the fortunes of our house,—
They said, We are the rose that drops its leaves.

TACUBA.

So sad ! you were more hopeful yesterday.
What gloomy news has come from Tezcuco ?

AÇALAN.

Oh ! Tacuba, we change from day to day.
Give us blue sky, a pleasant moving wind,
And cheery sight of flowers, forgotten all
Our troubles are : harder it is to grieve.
I am too childish, quick to weep and quick
To laugh again ; and then repentance comes,—
I am a woman,—conscience adds the sum
Of sorrows.   Oh ! I am most miserable.

TACUBA.

Am I not banished ?   I have glory seen
Fly from my capital in smoke and flame ;
Its temples desecrated.   But I live,
And shall regain my throne ; and so shall you
See Tezcuco when Guatemozin brings
Thy brother to his throne.

AÇALAN.

Coanaco,
Have you seen him of late?

TACUBA.

Ay, he is well.

AÇALAN.

Since driven from his throne he is so wretched !
First, wild with rage, with imprecating speech,
And gestures terrible to see, he stormed ;
Then he grew melancholy, and sat alone,
Moody, and gazed with fixed, despairing eyes ;
And lastly, from his sight he bade me part,—
I 'minded him too much of Tezcuco.
This loads my grief: to think Istrisuchil
A brother over-weights!   What constitutes
A brother?—blood,—a common parentage ?
Such bring us near together, and if foes
They open strife.   How is Istrisuchil,
My brother? we want other word for him.

TACUBA.

A comely stock may bear a warty branch,
That some unwonted freak of nature grows,

When form and color of the parent fail:
But this usurper of his brother's throne
Is linked to Cortés, and will fall with him.

ACALAN.

Will Cortés fail?

TACUBA.

       The menials of this palace
Outnumber thrice his men.   How can he stand?

ACALAN.

The Spaniards, ay; but Cortés grows in strength
By all our ancient foes, and, what is worse,
The powers of our throne unfriendly.

TACUBA.

            Name
It not, a brittle staff he leans upon:
They follow slavishly.   They fear the throne,—
It stands on loyal props, which, driven deep
Beneath the shifting quicksand hearts of men,
Are firm in custom: to sit thereon is safe.
Let one step down with trusting feet to walk
This fair but falsest ground,—men's selfish hearts,—
And he will sink and drown in treachery.

These Spaniards are the knot that ties them all;
We'll cut it.   Are they gods? We proved them men
When we revenged the slaughter of our friends.
We drove them hence.   I slew them with these hands.

Açalan.

In times like these our sex must trust your strength;
Sometimes a doubt born of our ignorance
Makes us to tremble of uncertainty.
We know our weakness: it is ever here,
Numbing the heart of hope; and it is here,
Tying with cords invisible our hands.
We cannot know what needed strength you have
To meet the evils fear is leading on.
Our arms are pliant stems of slender plants;
They cling and wreath the strong with fuller verdure;
We cannot bind with them; we win in th' calm,
Diviner wage, the tempest tears us down.

Tacuba.

Trust us: we reared these empires, and the hands
That built can keep.

> *Enter* Prince Tizoc (*unobserved*).

Açalan.

So sure: thou hast no fear?

TACUBA.

None, none. The waters over mine are deep;
But Mexico stands high, they will recede,
But not so rapidly that Guatemozin
May not, as with a wind, blow mightily
To mist and cloud, to fall in other deeps,
Their substance, whence they never will return,
And then for peace! O, Açalan, one kiss?

AÇALAN.

My Tacuba, for that one word, peace.
                              They observe TIZOC.

TACUBA.

                                        How,
Now, Prince, eavesdropping with a desp'rate face:
Meanest thou harm to us?

TIZOC.

                              Thou art unjust,
I suddenly came on thy privacy;
This open garden and all-seeing sun
Are gossips; blame thyself, not me.

AÇALAN.

                              Thy scowl?

TIZOC (*aside to* AÇALAN).

You ask me that ! (*aloud to* TACUBA).

　　　　　　　　My scowl? there is enough
To make the patient earth wrinkle her brow,
And shake with frenzy, that she's forced to bear
Upon her bosom such ingratitude.
The town of Chalco has deserted us ;
Cortés gives aidance to her treason by his arms ;
The King commands that thou, Lord Tacuba,
In this emergency, as is most fit,
Shalt lead our arms against these rebels.

TACUBA.
　　　　　　　　　What,

Has Chalco too rebelled !　Half-hearted slaves.
Jumping to Cortés' arms they'll meet instead
Our spears.　'Tis ever thus when dangers threat
That cowards fly, and selfish interest
Forgets the past, the generous provider,
Whose bounty battened it, for fear to lose
The merest fraction : but they shall eat dust ;
Be beggars for a crust of favor.

TIZOC.
　　　　　　　　　Ay,

But mouthing threats will win no battles.　Go
Thou to the king.

TACUBA.

Thy way belies thy words:
Thou art my enemy.

TIZOC.

Pardon, my lord,
My rough and ardent tongue; these Chalcoans
Have spoiled my temper for to-day.

TACUBA.

Lead on;
Let's to the king.

To AÇALAN.

Farewell.

Exeunt TACUBA *and* TIZOC.

AÇALAN.

I fear Tizoc:
That Tacuba was mine, I Tacuba's,
He knew not: I concealed my precious secret,
Not to allure, it was mine own—mine own.
I hate the man; I strove to quench his love
By ways as sure as water to quench fire;
But such a steam and sooty passion rises
Out o' him, he seems for very spite to woo.

Re-enter TIZOC.

TIZOC.

So ice may melt! I thought thee proud and cold,
And hoped by importunity to win.
So I have sought roses in Tacuba's
Garden.   Thou hast misused me.

AÇALAN.

It is false,

Foolish man.

TIZOC.

So, thou lovest Tacuba?

AÇALAN.

Enough of this, Sir Prince.   Thou art unfit
For ladies' company.

Exit AÇALAN.

TACUBA.

On thee, on thee,

My Lord of Tacuba.
                    Looking around suspiciously.
                            I am a babbler;
I cannot trust the tongueless earth with that.

2

SCENE II.—MEXICO.

A room in PRINCE TIZOC'S *house.*

Enter PRINCE TIZOC.

TIZOC.

And so she loves the Lord of Tacuba;
Nathless she shall be mine, shall lay her head
Upon my breast, look sweetly in my eyes.
'Tis grief that beautifies a woman's soul:
Her tears reveal within her heart a hoard
Of tenderness, as streams swifter with rains
Disclose the virgin gold.   Her love to grow
Must root itself in fear, a dread of loss,—
Ay, even loss, too rich a soil is bad;
Flatter a woman with continual joy
And love grows rank, all stalk and leaves.
No drought, no fruit: she must be starved to beg;
And when she begs, by love's quick providence,
With boundless wealth repays our charity;
And so would love, if Tacuba should die,
Feed with the worms?   No, no, love feeds on warm
And breath-moist lips, and sets his fire in th' eyes,
Not in the sockets of a skull.   I will be food.

Sweet Açalan, in poverty shall grip
The one sole morsel left of all to her.
All will be well if Tacuba but die.
(*Pondering.*)   It needs must be.   (*Calling.*)   Ho,
Attend me instantly !

Enter ATTENDANT.

Send me the slave I got to-day.

Exit ATTENDANT.

I bought

Him for his viciousness.   Intractable,
He must be harshly tamed : fear must persuade,
And interest enlarge obedience.
I'll practice on his vents of whims and humors,
Till, like a windy flute, he pipes my way.
First, to be cruel, and make him despair ;
Then offer freedom for his price ; twice bought,
Then twice my slave, the deed is doubly sure.

Enter TUNAL., *the slave.*

TIZOC *to* TUNAL.

Knowest thou who thy owner is?

TUNAL.

Thou art

He.

TIZOC.

Ay?

TUNAL.

The Prince Tizoc?

TIZOC.

　　　　　Thou knowest not
Thy owner yet.　Stand near to me,—so, so.
If I should sell thee, what would be thy fate?

TUNAL.

If twice I'm sold the law condemns to death.

TIZOC.

And carest thou to live?

TUNAL.

　　　　　Ay, sir, to live.

TIZOC.

Wilt thou obey my will, obsequious
As my shadow; be without identity;
A particle of earth lost in the soil

Of servitude, the mold which I shall till ;
An instrument without a thought but mine,
My hands shall use, without a feeling, worn,
Abused in using ?

TUNAL.   ·

Ay, my master.

TIZOC.

I

Shall see.   Bring me yon staff.

> TUNAL *brings the staff to* TIZOC, *who beats him
> with it, and then throws it away.*

Bring it to me

Again.

> TUNAL *brings it, and* TIZOC *beats him, and throws
> it away as before.*

Go, bring the staff again.

> TUNAL *brings it again, but when* TIZOC *goes to
> strike he seizes him and they struggle.*

TIZOC.

Unhand

Me, villain.   Help !   Help !   Help !

TUNAL.

I'll strangle thee.

Enter ATTENDANTS.

TIZOC.

Ha! Seize the slave and bind him fast with cords.

The ATTENDANTS *master and bind* TUNAL.

TUNAL.

Bind me—the cords may break—bind me with death;
I welcome death. What hold hast thou on me?
I will provoke thee, proud and cruel man.

TIZOC.

Ho, ho! (*To Attendants.*) Go, leave the slave alone
with me.

Exeunt ATTENDANTS.

If, when I tickle thee, thou art enraged
Beyond the trifling cause, what wilt thou do
When I thee cage as something wild,—a beast,—
And feed thee with the food we give to brutes;
And daily for amusement stir thee up,
And prick thee with my spear to see thee snarl,
And bite thy bars?

TUNAL.

I'll curse thee till I die.

TIZOC.

How camest thou a slave: so stout a heart
Should have fared better?

TUNAL.

What, against the State,
The frowns of heaven, and the fraud of man !
I was an husbandman ; unfruitful fields
And cloudless skies first taught me treachery,
And thrice my crops made fail.   The King's tax-man
Is never barren of his tribute ; though
A nation perish with a famine, food
Is in kings' houses, even some to waste.
Thrice him I paid my store ; when all was gone
He came again ; for want of evidence
To free me I was sold a slave, my wife
And children—

TIZOC.

Wife and children ! where are they ?

TUNAL.

Why wouldst thou know !   What have they done to thee.

TIZOC.

They shall be mine to torture in thy sight ;
That touches on the raw: thou wincest, ha !
Think you to lay your slavish hands on me,
And go unpunished ?   Shall death steal the purse
The almoner of misery, Revenge,
Has filled with pains to give in charity ?

TUNAL.

O, mercy, mercy ! why have I a heart,
To suffer with ? The beast forgets his young,—
Would I was one ; or stone insensible,
And laid beneath the feet of men, and worn,
And blown to indistinguishable earth.
O, master, pardon : look into thy heart,
Thou wouldst not patiently endure a wrong.

TIZOC.

Thou art a daring slave.   I am a prince.

TUNAL.

I will serve thee as more than all thy slaves ;
Anxious to do thy will as starving man
Hungers for food ; and quick to yield thy wish
While yet 'tis breathed, as tender grass to bend,
Wind-blown ; as particular as searching air
To find and fill up every space of duty ;
And I will bear thy treatment humbly, but—
Pity my wife and children.

TIZOC.

Thinkest thou
I have no purpose other than to play ?

I have no pity.   Thou art mine; thy life,
And what is dearer than thy life, are mine;
Ay, more is mine: to make thee free again;
Thy last estate happier than thy first.
What is a slave one more or less to me?
I'm rich in slaves—and yet among them all
None can I trust: a half-willed service robs
Me of my property.   Sell me thyself:
Sell me thy will, I'll pay thee well for it.
I saw thee in the Mart: thy scowling face
Brought none to buy,—I bought thee for that look;
Thou wert untamed and still had will.   Hark thou,
Thy business must be mine, thy life, thy hopes,
Thy fears be mine, and thine; I must be served,
Unmarred by cowardly or careless work,
So that the deed be done, as needs, well done,
Thou shalt be free again.
Is this your price?
Here is no room for gratitude or hate,
Or any mawkish feelings of the heart:
'Tis business, plain and sober traffic.   Think
Well on my words.   *He unbinds* TUNAL.

TUNAL.

Thou art upraising me
To make my fall the deeper.

TIZOC.

No, my man ;

I am no trifler.

TUNAL.

O, my master, free—
Be free once more ; to peril life and limb !
What is the labor ?   Life is liberty,
Death, freedom ! be the deed a fearful thing,
I will do it.

TIZOC.

Only to kill a man.
Faugh ! see the knave start at the thought.

TUNAL.

Nay, master ;

I will do it.

TIZOC.

Art thou a bowman skilled
To fly a shaft true to a little mark ?

TUNAL.

Ay, I have flown an arrow at the sky,
And whilst it fell have made another strike
It in mid air.

TIZOC.

'Tis well.   Attend my words,—
Go cautiously : we tread on cracking sticks,
And keep thy tongue as if a spear had made
It motionless.   To-morrow, with the Lord
Of Tacuba, I march against the Spaniards ;
With me thou goest ; what my purpose is
I will acquaint thee then.   Go, call my page.

     TUNAL *goes to the door and returns with a* PAGE.
(*To the Page.*)   Conduct this man into my armory,
Let him be armed one of my body-guard.

               Exeunt TUNAL *and* PAGE.
If he betrays me, what against my word
Is his—he dies, and if he fails he dies,—
O, I am safe.   My Lord of Tacuba,
Kiss her on the lips, sweet Açalan is mine :
For I shall send so fair a shaft, thy body
Will open lips and kiss thy life away.

SCENE III.—MEXICO.

Audience-room of the palace.

OYOT *in attendance.* AMBASSADORS *and others waiting an audience with the King.*

Enter AÇALAN.

AÇALAN *to* OYOT.

Doth not the King grant audience to day?

OYOT.

Your Highness is too early.

AÇALAN.

           Have you seen
The Lord of Tacuba?

OYOT.

           He is returned
From Chalco, and has audience to-day.

AÇALAN.

And who are these that wait? Methinks I know
Their faces: are they not from Tezcuco?

OYOT.

Ay.

AÇALAN.

I will go and speak with them.
    (*Approaching, and speaking to them.*)   Good sirs—

AMBASSADOR.

It is the princess.

AÇALAN.

        What news from Tezcuco :
How fares it with that city ?

AMBASSADOR.

        Madam, we
Are loath to tell it ; were the hopeless words
As bitter to the taste as gall 'n our mouths,
No sense could rebel more.

AÇALAN.

        You have no news :
Tidings of evil are not news to us.

AMBASSADOR.

We bear a letter Cortés sends the king.
                Enter TACUBA, *his arm bandaged.*

AÇALAN.

O, Tacuba, wounded, and sorely?

TACUBA.

No.:

Only a scratch in my arm.

AÇALAN.

Tell me all.

TACUBA.

We marched to Chalco, walled ourselves
Between the city and the coming foe;
Who, rushing on, astride the monstrous beasts
Of which they seem a part, struck on our line;
We stood the onset bravely, and they fell back,
As when one throws a stone against a rock,
Rebounding, and broken, it rolls away.
A second time they came, and I was hurt—
Most strangely wounded.

AÇALAN.

Strangely! tell me how.

TACUBA.

That strange, uncounted sense—instinctive fear,
Sniffed, like a deer that scents the tainted air,

The coming evil : quick I turned around ;
All in a flash I saw the bow full-drawn,
And back the levelled shaft the baleful eye,
And felt the arrow pierce.   I knew him not,
And never gave him cause to wish my death.

Açalan.

No cause to wish thy death !   Did'st thou not get
Thy wound in battle ?

Tacuba.

                    Ay ; but not from foe.

Açalan.

A friend, and not a foe ?

Tacuba.

                    Is this the work
Of friends ?

Açalan.

                    What troubles you ? thou answerest me
Such contradictions.

Tacuba.

                    I was thinking :—'twas
The slave of Prince Tizoc that wounded me.

AÇALAN.

What cause had he?

TACUBA.

None.

AÇALAN.

Knewest thou the man
In other times?

TACUBA.

I knew him not. It is strange.

AÇALAN.

Strange, or some enemy is back of him:
Tizoc—

TACUBA.

What means thy agitation?

AÇALAN.

Pardon,

O Tacuba,—dear Tacuba, it was—
My vanity.

TACUBA.

Thy vanity, Tizoc,
The garden, ay: he is unscrupulous,

And so beset with selfishness, the least
To stir the heart of man becomes in his
A mountain of complaints that load his reason
Until it breaks, and wild undoing rules.
No, no, they seized the slave ; Tizoc smote him,
But not to death, for he dissembled death ;
When we were driven by the enemy
Backward a space, he rose and fled to them.

Enter Tizoc.

Tizoc.

My Lord of Tacuba, I wish you sure
And quick recovery.

Tacuba.

           I thank you, Tizoc.

Tizoc.

The Princess Açalan, fair cousin, brightest
Of all the thoughts that poets sing of beauty
And loveliness incarned.   Gaze on, my lady.

Açalan.

Thou can'st not look me in the eyes.

Tizoc.

               They are
Too bright, and dazzle mine.

Açalan.

I know thee, Prince.

Tizoc.

Behold, my Lord, how she requites my service.

Açalan.

How knewest thou my thoughts?

Tizoc.

I know not now.

Açalan.

Unwary is thy tongue.   What service hast
Thou done?

Tizoc.

I smote the slave that wounded him.

Açalan.

That parried not the shaft.   Why magnify
So small a thing?

Tizoc.

'Twas love for Tacuba.

AÇALAN.

Thy love?

TIZOC.

Ay, love, and thou shouldst praise the hand
That was his helper.

AÇALAN.

Fair words; but, Prince Tizoc,
Thou art most false in this.

TIZOC.

Bitter, my lady;
For less men's lives are often perilous.

TACUBA.

The Prince Tizoc must not forget the due
Of loyal reverence, this princess's right.

TIZOC.

Must not? that speech I am unused to hear.

OYOT.

My lords, the king approaches, cease your strife.

Enter GUATEMOZIN, CULQUIL, *and other attendants.* GUATEMOZIN *ascends his throne; all
render obeisance.*

GUATEMOZIN.

My Lord of Tacuba, thou hast done well.

TACUBA, *approaching the throne.*

Your majesty, I grieve that my report
Was of defeat; we did what man could do.

GUATEMOZIN.

Be not down-hearted, for such victories
Surely defeat themselves, and such defeats
Shut up unbloomed our victory, as doth
A cold and passing storm delay a flower,
That will as surely burst its scentless husk,
And load the winds with all its treasured sweets.
The day comes not with lightning-flash to illume
The darkened earth, and startle us from sleep
With blinded eyes to blink the noonday glare
And painful blaze; the dawn doth softly come,
A salve to eyes: first shadows lighten, then
The rising sun—full day will come at last.

TACUBA.

Your majesty, 'twas by the wound I got,
Just when we stood opposed the foe, all strained
In every power to utmost extent

To hold against the tugging tide of war,
And the cry went up our general is killed.
As if a cord had snapped that hitherto
Had held us back, we in confusion 'whelmed
Upon the stormy sea of battle drove,
And all was lost.

TIZOC.

Your majesty, I grieve
He was a slave of mine whose treacherous shaft
Wrought our defeat.

AÇALAN.

Your majesty, I charge
That Prince Tizoc incited to this crime
His slave.

GUATEMOZIN.

What cause had he?   What evidence
Is there on which to rest so grave a charge?

AÇALAN.

He was his slave—and—

TIZOC.

Blush, my princess, I
Will spare thy modesty, and tell it all:

I loved this lady, won by charms she ranks
So highly that because she scorned my suit,
And knowing well the passion deep in me,
She thought the maddened lover sought revenge
Against his fortunate and envied rival,
And, measured by the jealous wrath such charms
Ought to have kindled in my heart, his death.

GUATEMOZIN.

Thy brutal sneer doth ill become thee, prince.

CULQUIL.

O king, I wot not what my duty is.
With deeds of loyal love I would thee serve,
And do no thankless work, myself great harm,
Coming between the friction of the Great,
Like corn 'tween grinding stones, all pulverized.

GUATEMOZIN.

Speak, thou art safe from harm.

CULQUIL.

This slave we seized,
And dragged him, struggling, to the rear ;
He stretched his arms to Prince Tizoc, and cried,
O master, save ! save me !

TIZOC.

But did I save?
Nay, to revenge.   Who smote the slave?   'Twas I.
He 'scaped by a hair.

AÇALAN.

The Prince Tizoc is wise.

GUATEMOZIN.

Prince, thou'lt be tried to prove thy innocence;
But if thy guilt be proved thou art to die:
For these suspicious fingers, that do here
Now point at thee, shall double in the fist
To strike.

OYOT.

Your majesty, an embassy
Awaits an audience, I understand,
With charge of weighty words.   The State demands,
By urgent pleas of peril in delay,
To bear.

GUATEMOZIN.

Let them approach; and, prince, more anon.
            The AMBASSADORS *approach the throne.*

CULQUIL (*aside*).

Look, Melancholy sends her children here.

AMBASSADOR.

O king, from Cortés we a letter bear.

GUATEMOZIN.

Downcast and shamed, your errand sorts with you.

AMBASSADOR.

To do this was the price of liberty,
We prisoners were.

GUATEMOZIN.

Give me the letter.
The letter is handed to GUATEMOZIN, *who glances over it.*
Now,
This blear and impudent eclipse would stare
The sun clean out of countenance and bring
Untimely night.   Thy scowling eyes may gaze,
But still he'll shine on us.

Reads aloud.

The past shall be
Forgotten,—those who injured me are dead.
The injury a robber has when one
Defends his own : ay, dead, and doth he think
To win our love by quickening revenge?

He reads again.

Only return to thy allegiance,

And all shall be forgiven, thy crown made sure.
O patience, calm my heart, it flutters like
A bird to fly at him,

   Throwing down the letter and leaving his throne.

      This hissing snake,
That comes so near her nest.   No, Montezuma,
More priest than soldier, conquered by a fable;
Trembler at lawless stars that rush on doom,
Am I: men are my portents, when I call
They come, and clothe the land in human verdure.
Cortés, thou boaster, come, and arrows deep
Shall cover thee as leaves the forest ground!
My country, O my mother! take back thine own,
For what I am thy love has made me; come
Thy danger in what form, if horrible,
With that worst agony, the will to do
Without the power; ay, be my strength and skill
As vain as pitch to quench destroying fire,
I willingly will give myself for thee.

OYOT.

What answer shall be made?

GUATEMOZIN.

    I am bent down,
But I will straighten like a bow that shoots.

OYOT.

I beg your majesty—

GUATEMOZIN.

Sound the alarm ;

Go call to arms.

OYOT.

I crave your majesty

To bear advice.

GUATEMOZIN.

What buzzing words are these ?
Wilt thou delay my vengeance ?

OYOT.

Your majesty's

Permission to discharge this embassy
With suitable defiance.

GUATEMOZIN.

Let them go :

I will not answer, but by silence, *him*,
'Thas fuller speech than words, which cage the thought
Within their bars ; but silence leaves the mind
Discourteously to itself to dart

On everything contempt engenders there.
I'll hear no more to-day: the audience
Is ended.   I must count my soldiers o'er,
And count them o'er again till I am calm.
My Lord of Tacuba, we will inspect
Our forces, and determine with what blows
These hammers of our throne shall fall to crash
The nutty heads whose cracking will be sweet.

ACT II.

SCENE I.—TEZCUCO.

Time, night. ANTONIO DE VILLAFANA'S *quarters.* *A storm is rising.* *Lightning flashes at the window.* ANTONIO *alone.*

> *Knocking heard at the door.*

ANTONIO.

Who's there? if friend, come in; if foe, come on.

> *Enter* MUÑOZ.

Welcome, Muñoz ; thou'rt early at our tryst.

MUÑOZ.

Prompt as a lover.

ANTONIO.

Wetted our friends will be.

MUÑOZ.

It matters not, their ardor 'll dry their clothes;
They are so hot in this, the flicker of
The lightning is to them a passing cloud
Athwart the moon.

ANTONIO, *going to the window.*

It is an earnest storm.
The gibbous moon no longer rules alone :

From out the caverns of yon mountain-cloud
Embers of intermittent fires suffuse
With her, and all the heavens brighter flame.
On come the breezy heralds of the blast,
Riding on dusty steeds adown the street ;
They flap the casements with their winding horns.

MUÑOZ.

'Tis time for storms : the lazy air of strict
Obedience, of smothering routine,
Sickens me.   Breathing kindred breath, awake,
Ye winds of passion ; blow these men as trees ;
Strip off their leaves, and crash their branches down ;
Work any ruin, only make us free.

A person is heard passing in the street, singing.

SONG.

The oak stands on the mountain-side,
Deep-rooted, firm, of iron heart,
And there the birds in shelter 'bide
When storms come down and lightnings dart.

He waves his arms, he calls the blast,—
Come fight, and wrestle for the day,
The brave old oak stands to the last,
And hurls the howling winds away.

ANTONIO.

That song had some coincidence in it.

MUÑOZ.

'Twas Farfan, more obsequious to Cortés
Than is yon lake to lighten to the sun;
He sees the coming storm, and shelter prates.
Yon hive of bees of Mexico is stirred,
They buzz in wrathful councils; go we there,
Such multitudes of stingers, roaring waves
Of poison will on us!
And go we must,
Unless we use this pause in Tezcuco
To rebel. Old Time is losing all his hair:
That gray forelock of his that's grasped so often
Grows thin of late—hairs drop like seconds. Ha!

ANTONIO.

To-night we must complete our plan of action.
'Tis time our friends were come.

MUÑOZ.

And they are here.

Enter BAMBA, JERONIMO, PEDRO, *and* FERNAN,
and other conspirators.

ANTONIO.

Comrades, your promptness presages your hearts;
Your stern demeanors great resolves foretell.
'Tis Cortés' death?

JERONIMO.

We are determined so.
Our wrongs composed become in us resolves
As such ingredients must make; good things
We mixed in his selfish pot till they have soured.
We sold our patrimonies, gave the gold
And our most cheerful service to this cause;
And what is brewed? wounds, rags, hungers, and
   thirsts.
Only our lives are left; he hazards these
As if they were no more than dice he rattles
To throw for fortune.

ANTONIO.

Then act ere they be cast.
Delay confesses weakness, 'tis the pause
For strength that comes between the lifted sword
Of weary fighter and his trembling stroke—
The time his foeman takes to run him through.
Success all hangs on Cortés' instant death;
While Cortés lives rebellion is betrayed.

BAMBA.

We must be circumspect; we know how bold
And cunning Cortés is.   I served with him
When you, Antonio, and others here
Obeyed Narvaez' lead.   Our deadly foes,
Ye landed on these shores, a thousand 'gainst
Barely three hundred men, to steal away
Our infant enterprise—a goodly babe
We cradled on our shields.   Attacked by night,
We were to you the prodigies of dreams;
With nightmared limbs ye stood till morn revealed
Our scant array with hardships overworn,
When, fired with shame, ye showed to rise against
Our victory, an easy thing to do;
But Cortés, by his arts, you captives made
To do his will.   That was a victory.
How gross become our arms when, by mere force
Of will and skilful move upon your fears
And hopes, ye did that willingly which else
Was not in bloody battle to compel.

ANTONIO.

We were cajoled, beaten with promises:
Sugar of words sweetened the bitter thing.

PEDRO.

Where is the gold he promised us?

JERONIMO.

In the eye,
Pedro, as much as thou canst carry there
And see; or in the ear, and wisdom hear.

ANTONIO.

Cortés is desperate: he knows escape
Lies only in a conquest of this land,
And that we know to be impossible.
Usurper, thief, the foe of every right,
Success alone will sheath th' avenging sword,
Less swings it with a doubly vengeful stroke;
Failure, that worst of sins, revenges wrong.
Ours is no case like his, we can return
Now, ere too late, to Spain.

JERONIMO.

Antonio,
None should be here but those with hearts like thine.

BAMBA.

I am with you: think not my caution meant
Half-hearted fellowship.

4

ANTONIO.

   Comrades, attend,
I have a plan, and beg your judgment on 't;
If fault there be, your wisdom for a better.
We will a packet bear to Cortés, when
At table he and his friends unwary sit,
Purport despatches instant, just arrived,
All rushing in as if to hear the news;
And as he reads, another message we,
With poniards, will inscribe upon his heart
To spell in purgatory. Cortés dead,
We speedily, with bloody daggers raised,
Will run, our eager voices clamorous
Of liberty and home, and bid all see
The blood of tyrant Cortés slain for them.

JERONIMO.

I see no fault in it; dost thou, Muñoz?

MUÑOZ.

None: it is clear as day of spectral doubts.

BAMBA, *at the window.*

The storm is past; no rain has fallen; calm,
The moon, sole mistress of the dewy air,

Illumes the night. (*Aside.*) I weary of this plot.
(*Aloud.*) I shiver; it grows cold.

ANTONIO, *to* BAMBA.

Come hither, let
A daring spirit chafe thy blood to warmth.

PEDRO.

Who joins with us? I am reluctant till
I know their edge and temper.

ANTONIO, *showing a paper.*

Read this list;
The names of many Cortés trusts are there.

PEDRO, *after reading.*

Ah! this assures us.

BAMBA.

Friends, I must retire:
I still am servitor of recent wounds,
And they command to rest.

ANTONIO.

You are not well;
But rest thyself, we need thy trusty sword.

Exit BAMBA.

MUÑOZ, *to* ANTONIO.

Art sure Bamba is trusty?

ANTONIO.

                    Ay; he lacks
Only the nerves of health; his heart is ours.

MUÑOZ.

We all are ready,—when are we to strike?

JERONIMO.

Strike now; to-night.

ANTONIO.

          That is impossible;
We first must send a message to our friends,
And fix a time when all shall come together.

MUÑOZ.

That can be done to-night; to-morrow, then,
Let it be done.

ANTONIO.

What say you, comrades?

ALL.

Ay.

ANTONIO.

Then let us part, I will inform the rest
Our plan, and all the very time to act,
When liberty shall hear our daggers knock
And ope her doors to us.   Jeronimo,
Fernan, and Pedro, ye will tarry here,
And aid me in this work.

CONSPIRATORS, *going out.*
Good-night.

ANTONIO.

Good-night.

Exeunt all except ANTONIO, JERONIMO, FERNAN,
and PEDRO.

SCENE II.—TEZCUCO.

The same night.   In front of RAMON'S *quarters.*
A table set for drinking, lighted by a flambeau.
The moon is shining on a part of the scene.

Enter, from within, RAMON, FARFAN, *and* PANFILIO.

RAMON.

Be seated, friends.
   They sit down; then RAMON, *holding up a bottle :*
         Farfan, your glass, and yours,
Panfilio.   *After filling all round, holding up his own.*
   See ye that sleeping flame,
Unbottled light : old Xeres brings the sun
Of Spain to warm us.   *They drink.*

PANFILIO.

   It takes me home again.

FARFAN.

Who loiters?
   RAMON.

   None.

FARFAN.

Here are four seats, four cups,
And but we three.

RAMON.

A fashion I was taught
At home.   They are the chance guest's seat and cup.

Enter BAMBA.

RAMON, *to* BAMBA.

Wilt thou, to honor us, sit at our board?

BAMBA.

I will; but truly you more honor me.

PANFILIO.

Ramon, thy custom has some hazard in 't.

RAMON.

Whoever comes, him must I ask to eat.

BAMBA.

What do ye mean?

PANFILIO.

Thou hast the chance guest's seat,
Another might have come and been unwelcome.

RAMON.

This custom lends to my sincerity
Nothing, Bamba, of truth, if none had been
Thou welcome art.

BAMBA.

'Tis a fair courtesy.

RAMON.

There is a story of my ancestor.
One day he dined in state, his table brave
With plate, rich viands, wines the costliest,
His guests in silks and velvets.   Every seat
Save one, the chance guest's, filled, when at the door
A beggar craved for alms.   My great-grandsire
Bade him be seated in the vacant chair,
A wan and weary man, with naked feet,
And clothed in rags : strange guest for such a feast.
The guests, amazed, drew back their silken selves,
As if they feared to soil their splendid robes.
His trembling hands spilled on the cloth the wine
Ere he had tasted it ; he crumbed the bread,
And left it on his plate, too weak to eat,
All while he not so much as raised his eyes.
At last he rose, and when he reached the door
He turned and looked upon his empty seat,

And then was gone.   All looked,—a golden cup
Filled to the brim with wine, a wafer on
A golden plate, stood at the chance guest's seat.
They say it was our Lord, who did not need
Our bread, but gave his body bread for us.

PANFILIO.

A monkish legend.

RAMON.

Nay, I had it from
My father; also, it is handed down,
And I confirm it by one instance proved.
What man or woman fills our chance guest's seat
Thenceforth, as if inspired direct from heaven,
Must lead a better life.   This knave was rich,
Extortionate, and proud; he gave his goods
To feed the poor, returned to every one
What was his due, and died a holy monk.

FARFAN.

Surely Bamba is caught in Heaven's trap.

PANFILIO, *calling.*

Bamba!

PANFILIO, *to the others.*

By all the saints, it works on him!
His eyes, inturned, look on a memory.

RAMON, *to* BAMBA.

Bamba!

To the others. He faints; give him a cup of wine.
Touching him. Bamba!

BAMBA, *starting to his feet.*

O holy Jesu, look not on me!
I am—you stare at me! What did I say?
Nothing? I am not well yet of my wounds.
Good friends, my mind is weak of late, and all—
No matter. Did I say aught? Fool, fool! Forgive
Me, friends; you see I rave. I must to bed.
My fever has returned, and fills my veins
With misery.

RAMON.

Thou canst not go alone?

BAMBA.

Alone! alone? no; not alone.   PANFILIO *offers.*
                                    Not thou,
Panfilio. Ay; 'lone. (*Staggering.*) You see I walk
With steady steps. Ramon, thou wilt excuse.

RAMON.

Ay, thou art sick.

PANFILIO.

Thy strength is traitor to

Thy will.　Let——

BAMBA.

Traitor?　I a traitor?　Oh!

Thou shalt not say it with impunity,

Though I be shadow of my former self.

Draw.

*He draws his sword; the others arise, and do the
same.*

BAMBA.

(*Striking at* PANFILIO.)　That, and that.

RAMON.

Panfilio, hold! hold!

Bamba is crazed; do but defend thyself.

BAMBA.

Oh, madness!　　　　　*Exit* BAMBA, *rushing off.*

PANFILIO.

Shall I after him?

RAMON.

No, no;

'Twould cross him to no good.　Best let him go

To cool alone.　We must not mar with strife

Our peaceful ease, the sweet vacation war's
Rough school allows, the rest that strengthens us
For sternest work. Sit down again, and let
The clouding dust of evil passions sink,
And leave the crystal of our former selves.
Come drink success to Cortés, it is near.

FARFAN, *after all drinking.*

Things go apace, the ships at last are launched;
We soon will be in Mexico again.

PANFILIO.

'Tis wonderful, think on't, that dreadful night
We fled from there. It was the blackest night
That ever quenched with clouds the light of stars.
I had to feel my foe before I struck,
Fearing he was a friend. We got so mixed,
'Tween strokes and prayers I fought, and hell was there
Without its fires to minish horror with
Foreseen destruction; 'twas above, below;
This side, that side, everywhere; shrinking, stopping,
Turning, as thought spun round from fear to fear,
I reached the land. That fatal causeway comes
At times across my mind, ever the same
Mad, jumbled terror. Let us drink again,
It has spoiled the wine I had.

RAMON.

We had one hope,
That to escape, for conquest was to us
Impossible.   We knew not Cortés then.
These ships we launched to-day, in distant forests
Hewn, borne by willing friends o'er leagues of moun-
  tains;
A labor Hercules might have sweat o'er,
Cortés, more god-like, finishes.

FARFAN.

He is
Of perfect force; a fortress of expedients.
I marvel at him.   No misfortune daunts,
But strengthens more, for that as yet has broke
Only our swords, but not his head, which seems
To rally more, as other help is lost,
An army forth invincible of plans,
To counterplot with fate.   He fails of nothing.

PANFILIO.

And yet we have skulkers and cowards here
That murmur 'gainst him.

FARFAN.

　　　　Friends, draw near to me;
We might be heard.　You know Antonio?
　　　They converse in an undertone.　Re-enter BAMBA,
　　　at one side.

BAMBA.

Thrice have I stood before his door, and thrice
The hand I raised to gain admission knocked,
Not pleading there, but on my heart with terrors
That come between my penitence and shame.
I can confess to heaven, but to man,—
We are too much alike; that which I fear
Is by that likeness made a judge most harsh;
Condemns without defence, for what defence
Has conscience 'gainst itself?　I must confess.
O misery, to be entangled thus!
Will I not be the means to foil this plot?
Take courage his, Cortés', deliverer.
My crime destroys my manhood!　There's no lie
More false than that we lie with to ourselves.
　　　　　　　　　　　Exit BAMBA.

FARFAN.

Did ye not hear a noise?　I thought I saw
A haggard face instant in yon moon-ray.

RAMON.

'Twas nothing.   Come, Panfilio, a toast.

PANFILIO.

Here's to the wish that nearest is our hearts ;
May it a full cup be, and drunken empty.

They drink.

PANFILIO, *holding the cup bottom upwards.*

See, every drop is down ; would ye hear mine ?

RAMON.

Some castle in New Spain, you fancy real.

PANFILIO.

The only castles in the air are clouds,
And their most wholesome waters nourish us,
And pleasure life, so shall my wish prevail.

RAMON.

Some clouds rain skyward, fade into the blue.

PANFILIO.

A sign that promises no storms are near.
I shall obtain a great estate by grant

For service rendered ; with my share of gold
Build me a country-seat ; buy slaves to bear
Life's cares away, while I enjoy its pleasures.

FARFAN.

Thy blood will sleep ; eager old age will leave
The beaten path, hobbling, cross-cut thy life.
Not so with me ; when this campaign is o'er
I shall be off to newer fields of glory.

RAMON.

Brave words, brave heart.

PANFILIO.

The wine has gone to sleep,
And so should we.

FARFAN, *rising.*

The morrow brings the march,
Perhaps a battle-field.

PANFILIO, *rising.*

Your arm, Farfan.

RAMON.

Stay, comrades, welcome goes not with the wine.

FARFAN.

Panfilio, we are uncourteous.

PANFILIO.

Nay,
We do not go because the wine is gone.

RAMON.

I blame you not.   Good-night.

Severally going.
Good-night.   Good-night.

SCENE III.—TEZCUCO.

The same night.   A room in CORTÉS' *quarters.*

Enter CORTÉS.

CORTÉS.

The earth's calm confidence of strength disdains
The lightnings, storms, and tremors of her frame
That harm the unrevengeful hills and vales:
Content to hide her hurt with fruitfulness,

5

And win redeeming beauty from a wound ;
So I would turn defeat to victory.
They thought us gods, allegiance gave our king,
They decked our arms, and crowned our heads with
      flowers.
Were we deceived ? Was it for sacrifice ?
Or did contact reveal humanity
Ungodly, and credulity revenge
Itself with our overthrow? That saddest night
A harping memory lives. I strove for power
By peaceful arts, that leave no rankling wounds
To linger civil wars ; the sword unsheathed
Must never bloodless to the scabbard turn.
This dynasty will not let go its power
With every fortress levelled to the plain ;
Its armies mown as by a pestilence,
Men's fierce and obdurate hearts must broken be,
Their wills be beaten down, their hopes made fail,
And all the bolts and bars of custom broken ;
Society disrupt, its members cast,
Like bursting waters, 'broad, and then reborn,
The State may rise, and only know the past
An alien chronicle, so changed and new
Its outer powers and inner potencies.

                Knocking heard at the door.

Who knocks? It was the wind. Ah! I will strike
With mailed hand on Fame till every bolt
And hinge shall shake within their portal seats.
If there is left to man in all this world
Of unrewarded worth, illusive hopes,
And where success is like a cagéd eagle
Pining his native freedom, losing strength
And beauty, one desire that's near fulfill'd,
It is to stand before the eyes of men,
As he who laid his sword within the warp
Of destiny, and held it woven there
Eternal as Orion's starry blade,
Which out no arm may draw, or it will cut
A gap in nature, high heaven's law be broke,
And chaos rule the darkened void again.

　　　　　There is knocking again at the door.

It was a knock, and something strange in it ;
I must not be unwary.

　　　　　Drawing his sword and opening the door.
　　　　　Enter, friend.
　　　　　　　　Enter BAMBA.

BAMBA, *seeing the sword, and falling on his knees.*

Mercy, great Cortés ; slay me not. O, mercy !

CORTÉS.

Pshaw, man, I was but looking to my arms,
Rough used of late, what need of armorer's skill
They had.   What means this shaking of thy limbs?
Thy pallid, trembling lips?   Arise and speak.

BAMBA, *rising.*

I fear myself, and thee, and everything ;
I have been sick, and tortured by the wounds
I got the night we fled from Mexico.
Rememberest thou the final struggle on
The fatal causeway ; in the press of men
Foe mixed with friend, and on the slippery edge
We fought, a stalwart warrior seized thy foot,
I stooping, with a blow, cut off his arm?
That stoop lost me my fence, and I was wounded.

CORTÉS.

Nay, the night was dark.   We oft in peril were.

BAMBA.

I hoped thou hadst remembered it.   Ah me !

CORTÉS.

What ails thee, man ?

BAMBA, *again kneeling.*

    Mercy ! I have been sick,
Let this decrepit thing, my body, tell.
What wonder that my mind and heart gave way,
And I reviled the poor reward I had,
And longed for home with no way there to go !
When thus dispirited, there came a man
Who harped upon my sufferings, greater woes
That were to come, and step by step I was led
To join with him and others to—— (*pausing.*)

CORTÉS.

     To what ?
Conspiracy ? Speak, sir.

BAMBA, *rising.*

     Ay, to conspire
Thy death, that we to Cuba might return.
To-morrow they will come.

CORTÉS.

    Who is this man ?

BAMBA.

Antonio de Villafana.

CORTÉS, *calling.*

Ho, there,

Within. (*To* BAMBA.) I will attend
thee presently.

Enter a soldier.

(*To the soldier.*) Go, bid the Captain of the Guard,
in my name,
Bring here four Alguazils, and wait my will.
Be quick, and let thy feet the silence chide
Of sleepy night with clamorous speed.

Exit soldier.

(*To* BAMBA.) Come,
I will examine you concerning this,
In privacy, with closer scrutiny.

Exeunt CORTÉS *and* BAMBA.

SCENE IV.—TEZCUCO.

The same night.   A street.

Enter ISTRISUCHIL, *and other* TEZCUCANS, *his followers.*

ISTRISUCHIL.

We march to-morrow; Mexico will fall,
And I be firmly throned.   I am no king,

Forsooth, usurper, traitor ; by this arm
I took more from my father's loins than all
My brothers ; I am king, and by my might
I'll write my title in that city's ruins.

Enter TUNAL, *passing.*

A TEZCUCAN.

My lord, the slave that fled from Mexico
Is passing.

ISTRISUCHIL.

Call him to me.

The TEZCUCAN, *to* TUNAL.

Whither so fast ?
Stay thou, the Lord Istrisuchil would speak
With thee.

TUNAL *approaches them.*

ISTRISUCHIL.

Thou wert the slave of Prince Tizoc ?

TUNAL.

I was, my lord.

ISTRISUCHIL.

What caused this enmity
Between Tizoc and Tacuba?

TUNAL.

The scowls
Of Prince Tizoc I heard commented on
Among his followers: those of his house
Had heard him when alone, as was his wont,
Mutter and talk; they said he was in love
With Princess Açalan; that Tacuba
Was favored more than he.

ISTRISUCHIL.

Ha! ha! my sister!
Thy sparkling eyes could ruin Mexico
If all our foes would fall in love with thee,
And fight among themselves.   Saw you my brother
Coanaco?

TUNAL.

He was with us.

ISTRISUCHIL.

At Chalco?

TUNAL.

Ay.

ISTRISUCHIL.

Ha! and I not there.   How did he look—
Gloomy?

TUNAL.

He did, my lord.

ISTRISUCHIL.

Ha! ha! and pale?

TUNAL.

He was, my lord.

ISTRISUCHIL.

Ha! ha! and did he gnaw
His lip this way?

TUNAL.

He did, my lord.

ISTRISUCHIL.

Ha! ha!
I know Coanaco: that was his way
When we were children, and I took his toys,
And beat him, if he fought to get them back.
(*Going.*)   Come on, you shall be of my followers,
And free from this day forth.   Poor Coanaco!

SCENE V.—TEZCUCO.

The same night. ANTONIO'S *quarters.*

ANTONIO, JERONIMO, PEDRO, *and* FERNAN *sitting at
a table.*

JERONIMO.

'Tis settled then Antonio shall give
The packet, and the signal when to act,
And we will gather round like flies a spot
Of honey, and strike.

ANTONIO.

Hist! What noise is that?

Enter CORTÉS *suddenly, with officers and soldiers.*

CORTÉS.

Arrest these men, save Villafana, all;
With him I wish a private conversation;
Detail a force to guard the three to prison.

JERONIMO, PEDRO, *and* FERNAN *are arrested, and
taken from the room.*

CORTÉS (*to* ANTONIO).

Antonio de Villafana——

> ANTONIO *takes a paper from the table, and tries to swallow it;* CORTÉS *seizes him; they struggle.*

                    Yield,
Thou villain, yield that paper, spit it out;
I'll have it though I rive thy trunk in twain,
And tear it from thy belly.

> CORTÉS *obtains the paper.*

CORTÉS (*to soldiers*).

                    Seize this man!

> *The Alguazils and soldiers arrest* ANTONIO.

CORTÉS (*to* ANTONIO).

Antonio de Villafana, I,
Before these gentlemen, and officers
Empowered to execute the laws, do charge
That thou most foully hast conspired our ruin,
Enticed more worthy men to join thy plot.
Thou hast been taken in the very act;
Yet speak, thou shalt not be condemned unheard.

ANTONIO.

You have the proof; what need I answer thee?

CORTÉS.

He has confessed ; haste ye, and hale him hence ;
Let him be shriven, and his peace be made
With heaven, for ere to-morrow's sun shall rise
His peace with earth must be.   Let not his life
Beyond its absolution last one hour.

Exeunt all but CORTÉS.

That precious list !   Who are my enemies ?
(*Opening the paper.*) Mouthed with that villain's slime.

He reads.

Now, never more
Let face of man be fair, and outward sign
Of what his heart contains, since treachery
And quick ingratitude have changed their fronts,
And meet us daily, look us in the eyes
As honesty itself.   This man I trusted,
And this, and this,—and in such company,
The offal of the camp.   Some feared, some hated,
Some loved.   Oh, love, thou juggler of the heart !
How can I rise above calamity ?
To lose these men would maim of limb the body
Of which I am the head.   Is there no cure,
Unless I lame myself; no folly, trait
Of human nature, simple of the heart,
To bring return of health ?   (*Pausing in meditation.*)

There is a weakness
That comes of knowledge, when we lack the means
To do what reason 'proves, which wisdom warns
Us to forego, whilst wrongs and righteous wrath
Pursue the doubtful will to drive to it.
A friend may be a fool, and thus a foe,
A foolish enemy better than friend.
To make my foe my friend I must deceive
Him to believe he's trusted ; scrupulous,
No word or sign betray I know the deep
That is betwixt us, which fair words and trusts,
But seeming fair and trusting, must o'erbridge.
He knows the gulf, but thinks I know it not,
And chuckles at my folly.   (*Pausing in thought.*)
          They are mine ;
I will conceal my knowledge of their crime,
Declare Antonio alone in guilt;
The others, freed from fear of instant death,
And eager to escape suspicion, will
Back to their duty ardently.   (*Tearing the paper.*)
          It is torn,
But not the record written on my mind,
Nor shall they go unwatched from this day forth.
In duty's ways good habits may return,
And treason be a thing to horror them.

SCENE VI.—TEZCUCO.

Early dawn. An open square. ANTONIO *is seen hanging from a beam fastened in an upper window.*

Enter MUÑOZ.

MUÑOZ.

O, such a night of horrors have I passed!
Awake, asleep, again awake and asleep;
The native hold upon my will all gone
In riotous rebellion of my dreams.
Rebellion, treason,—how these words become
The catch-words of my mind.   I have a qualm
From over-eating; treason is at court;
In sooth, base coin in the treasury;
King Reason is dethroned, and all my wits
Are regicides.   I dreamed that I was hanged;
My neck is stiff of it.   Ha!   What is that?
By the sword of Damocles, that spider dream
Has left its cobwebs in my brain; or no,—
It is Antonio!   Antonio!
Antonio is hanged! and we are lost.
They come to seize me—no, a terror cried

In m' ears, they come!   I am all desperation,
I must away, and warn the rest of danger.

Exit MUÑOZ.

Enter JERONIMO, PEDRO, *and* FERNAN, *released from
prison.*

PEDRO.

No clue was found, or why were we discharged?

FERNAN.

And when the jailer curtly made us free,
So certain was I that he came to hale
Me to the judge, my prison was a home
From which he forced me; even now I fear
My senses lie.

JERONIMO, *seeing* ANTONIO.

Look there!

PEDRO.

Who has been hanged?

FERNAN.

It is Antonio!

JERONIMO.

O, horrible
Extinguishment, and utter darkness come!

FERNAN.

Yon whirlwind's sheaf, must we be garnered there!

PEDRO.

We are distraught; it cannot be.

JERONIMO.

It is,
And we are free, and there our secret is.

PEDRO.

Emblazoned to the day!

JERONIMO.

Yon charnel-house,
The skull where dead men's thoughts sepulchred are,
Our secret buries; or why were we freed?

FERNAN.

Away, and let us tell the others what
Befell last night; we must be on our guard.

Exeunt all.

Re-enter MUÑOZ, *and enter other* CONSPIRATORS *with him.*

Muñoz.

See, there he hangs.

A Conspirator.

Where did you say?

Muñoz.

See, there.

Conspirator.

O, this is hell!

Second Conspirator.

How can we save ourselves?

Muñoz.

O curse the paltering fool; he might have known
That instant action should have followed thought;
The winds will bruit abroad such secrets, being
The servitors of heaven.

Enter Jeronimo, Pedro, *and* Fernan, *cautiously.*

Jeronimo, *in a subdued voice.*

Hist, Muñoz,

Muñoz.

Muñoz, *answering.*

We all are friends.

6

JERONIMO, *pointing.*

See there—see there,
Yon dreadful exclamation point of fear
To us !

MUÑOZ.

See it ? I've gazed on it so long
There is a hanging man before my eyes
Wherever I may look.   I see one now
Upon thee, man.

JERONIMO.

Pluck up thy courage, things
Are not so bad.   Last night we were with him,
When Cortés came with soldiers, seized us three
And had us 'prisoned, and this morn released
Without a question asked or reason given.
We come and find Antonio is hanged.
Have we the more, or less, to fear from this ?

MUÑOZ.

O, this arouses my benumbed heart !
It bodes us well ; and all the evidence—
If he were hanged for treason—must have been
Wholly against himself ; for never yet,
Since Satan fell from heaven, has treason had
A respite.

PEDRO.

I cannot believe in safety.

MUÑOZ.

I do, because it seems impossible.
'Tis Luck.   When all our calculations fail,
This little rosy sprite, fat as a dumpling,
And just as sensible as a lump of dough,
Comes plump amongst us, and sets all a laughing.
This will cause men to watch each other; see
To it ye cast in all suspicious eyes
Pretentious dust of loyalty; assume
A careless mien, and cheer Antonio's doom.

JERONIMO.

You counsel well, and we must hold no tell-tale
Intercourse.

MUÑOZ.

Some one comes; away, away.
                    (*Exeunt all except* MUÑOZ.)

Enter soldiers, and MUÑOZ *mingles with the crowd;*
then enter FARFAN *and* PANFILIO.

PANFILIO, *to* FARFAN.

You judged the traitor rightly.

FARFAN.

Ay, he was
Always a grumbler; treason grafts the best
On such a stock.

PANFILIO.

The gallows-tree is bare
Of leaves and fruit; at night, by darkness sunned,
Fed by a drought of every worthy deed,
A sapless branch has grown: a direful sum
Of contradictions, yet reality.

SOLDIER.

Was he alone?   Surely one man is nothing.

FARFAN.

He was alone; Cortés has so announced.

PANFILIO.

But others must have known——

MUÑOZ, *interrupting.*

Down with all traitors!

PANFILIO.

Up by a rope, I say ; up by the neck.

FARFAN.

Muñoz, they tell me you are chosen one
To serve aboard the ships.

MUÑOZ.

            Ay, that is my sore ;
I have been drafted for a common sailor ;
An old hidalgo ! I to pull at ropes,
To smell of tar and pitch !

FARFAN.

            And yet, Muñoz,
You trim your sails.

PANFILIO, *to* MUÑOZ.

           Thy neck will pull a rope
Some day, and spite thy hands, if thou rebelest.

                    Enter CORTÉS.

CORTÉS.

Go, call Muñoz to me.

MUÑOZ, *turning away.*

            He wants me.

PANFILIO.

Here
He is. Muñoz, the General.

MUÑOZ.

I come.

MUÑOZ *approaches, and salutes* CORTÉS.

CORTÉS.

Take twenty men, and scout the country south
Not more than seven leagues. Report to me
With liberal haste, finding the enemy
Are anywhere in force, what possible
Menace there is to us. Be cautious, not
Too bold ; risk no encounter : they'll not dare
Attack unless they are most strong in numbers ;
Acquit thyself as worthy of my trust.

MUÑOZ.

I will, I will ; if I neglect my duty,
Then hang my treason there (*pointing to* ANTONIO).

Exit MUÑOZ.

CORTÉS.

Soldiers, we march
On Mexico, and there awaits an empire
Glorious as all our earthly wishes make ;

So broad that every several one of us,
Without the elbow jostling of our rights,
Or losing by another's gain of power,
Can hold of office, rank, and wealth as much
As his good sword can win.

SOLDIERS, *shouting.*
　　　　　　　　Long live our leader !

CORTÉS.
We march to-day ; go to your companies.

ACT III.

SCENE I.—MEXICO.

A room in the palace. AÇALAN *and* QUEEN TECU-ICHPO *sitting by an open window.* AÇALAN *is working on a piece of embroidery.*

AÇALAN, *holding up the embroidery.*

There, it is done; and O, I am so glad!

QUEEN.

Why did you tire; it is so beautiful!
To see it grow, the nestling of thy hand,
To be a radiant bird, were joy enough.
This scarlet cardinal, with open beak,
Darting to catch the gemmy bug, is life
Caught in the mirror of thy tapestry,
To fly unweariedly.

AÇALAN.

Is it a fancy?
Is there not some suggestion in the bird
To call my brother's face?

QUEEN.

                              Istrisuchil's?

AÇALAN.

Ay.

QUEEN.

From the beak, and cruel eye it comes.

AÇALAN.

When nearly done I saw it, and I bore
The tortures of the thoughts it moved in me
As not beyond my strength; they grow too great;
I give it thee; take it away.

                    Handing the embroidery to the QUEEN.

                              He was
My terror when a child, and never has
His cruel boyhood softened in the man.

QUEEN.

Do not give way to gloom; the time is near
When Guatemozin will restore the throne
Of Tezcuco its rightful king.   Look thou
Between the parting of neighboring walls,
And see the placid lake; its waters stop
At Tezcuco; were we upon some summit

We might behold thy home.   When parted from
Our friends, to see them distant, know them safe,
We, partly happy, wait until we meet.

Açalan.

Thither my eyes have daily turned, and looked
So longingly.   .
Queen.

    See yon strange and distant shapes,
White spots upon the waves?   I think they move.

Açalan.

A boat would vanish there; what can they be?

Queen.

I fear they are our foes.

Açalan.

         See! see! they move!
And widen like waterfowl flying out.

Queen.

They must be Spanish ships; such Cortés built
When he my father's guest was; winged like birds,
With sails the wind blew on, they swept along.

          Enter an Attendant.

ATTENDANT, *to the Queen.*

The Prince Tizoc desires an interview.

AÇALAN.

The Prince Tizoc.   O, let me go.

QUEEN.

                                        Nay, child,
Thou must remain ; thou art unjust to him ;
Let pardon hear the gentle argument
Of hapless love.   If he had loved thee less
He would have had the greater calmness ; but
It maddened him ; cruel is love outraged.
(*To* ATTENDANT.)   Admit the Prince.
                                        Exit ATTENDANT.

AÇALAN.

                        Thy wishes are my laws ;
Only what simple courtesy may grant,
The stubborn injury of pride may yield.
                                        Enter TIZOC.

TIZOC, *to the* QUEEN.

(*Kneeling.*)   Madam, a boon ; I am a suppliant,
An importuner of thy graciousness.

QUEEN.

If it infringe no duty, work no wrong,
Nor burden foolishly my free consent,
Thou hast it.

TIZOC.

Plead for me this injured Princess
To pardon what my gross and treacherous pride,
Dethroning me, my heart's own queen misruled
To my disgrace and loss of her dear favor.

QUEEN.

That I have done.

AÇALAN.

Prince, thou art false.

TIZOC.

Ay, false,—
False to my happiness, but true to thee.

AÇALAN.

Didst thou not publicly insult me?

TIZOC.

Would
My tongue were palsied in my mouth ere I
Had wronged thee.

AÇALAN.

'Tis in service of thy heart
Thou wouldst be dumb, but full of evil thoughts,
Like dammed waters, but the deeper for 't.

TIZOC.

My heart is torn away, and gone forever.

AÇALAN.

Then thou art heartless in professing it.

TIZOC.

What shall I say?   Madam, persuade her heart
To gentleness.

QUEEN.

Dear Açalan, forgive.
A smile is better than a frown for all:
It even smoothes the wrinkles out of age,
Makes fair the homeliest; and when 'tis thine
It is the perfect finish of the face.

TIZOC.

Nay, frowns, by her prevailing loveliness,
Are angry charms that torture while they dazzle.

AÇALAN.

I could forgive, if I alone were harmed ;
Thou art the enemy of Tacuba.

TIZOC.

But he believes me innocent, and so
The king, and all the court, save you.

AÇALAN. .

Not now ;

I may forgive, but cannot yet forget.

An alarm is sounded.

QUEEN, *running to the window.*

The ships ! the ships ! and see our fleet of boats
Does hide the water with their multitude :
They go to meet them.

TIZOC.

Now the long delayed,
But surely coming trial of our strength
Is near.

AÇALAN.

And, Prince, thou shouldst be at thy post,
Not hiding here.

TIZOC.

I go ; and none can say
That Tizoc counts the purchase of old age
To be desired above the life that death
Exchanges glory on the battle-field.

(Aside.)

A siege within a siege : though fail the one,
I'll stake my all the other shall be won.

Exit TIZOC.

QUEEN, *to* AÇALAN.

Do you not feel a trembling like a chill
To creep and make thy body insincere?
Within our homes we hitherto have dwelt
In peace, no sound of war has reached our ears:
For we have only known its peaceful shows,
The march of gaudy soldiers, and their songs
Of triumph: now the battle's bloody fragments,
The dead and wounded men, will fill our streets.
To feel a constant dread uncertainty
Of final victory, a fear of ruin,
Our lives will be a restless misery.
Ah me ! to live upon a battle-field.

AÇALAN.

I tremble, but no fear is in the tremor :
The tender nestlings tremble in the wind,

But not for fear; the watchful, anxious thought
For those I love, and fate of things is pain,
And weariness of heart.

QUEEN.

       The penalty
Of greatness is ours to bear. O ! that we—
The king and I—some private subjects were,
To know the troubles only proper to
That station. I too private am to self,
Too subject to my heart for these great cares
That centre in a king, and make his will
A nation's thought, a nation's wrongs his pain,
The suffering that robs my right to him:
I get no room in his filled heart.

AÇALAN.

        Have care ;
The king comes here.

       Enter GUATEMOZIN.

GUATEMOZIN.

    All's done that can be done ;
Constant unto one purpose, as are roots
That thread and lace the elemental mould,
To find and draw up all the strength therein,

Have I, to thoughtless minds, the idle flower
That blooms upon the palm of state, the crown,
And ornament of all, been through the crude
And hidden substance of the nation's strength;
Nothing so small but I have treasured it.
If anything 's amiss, 'tis in this head,
Not in my heart.   They come; away reserve:
I leave the school-room of my cabinet,
Where I have conned my task to weariness,
To breathe again free air of battles.   Ah!
'Tis like to happiness.

QUEEN.

                         Art thou so happy;
Glad of this war?

GUATEMOZIN.

                    Thou understandest not.
Have you not noted how, since I am king,
What patient labors I have striven with,
O'ertaxing mind and body, lest that which
Is necessary be overlooked, and we
Made fail for want of preparation; what
So full I have been of, that I have robbed
My heart of its own joys, losing myself,
That others may be saved from lasting woe.
Wilt thou not pardon my neglect of thee?

7

QUEEN.

I pardon all for one kind word.

GUATEMOZIN, *pointing to the window.*

See yonder;
The people crowd the roofs, and wave their arms,
And gaze upon the lake.   The enemy—

A great shout is heard; all run to the window.

QUEEN.

Look! horror! look!

AÇALAN.

They run us down; like knives
They cut our boats in twain.

QUEEN.

The water 's full
Of drowning soldiers.

GUATEMOZIN.

Ha! we are o'ermatched;
I must draw off our fleet, and let them land,
And then. . . . .

Exit GUATEMOZIN.

QUEEN, *embracing* AÇALAN.

O, Açalan, didst thou not see
Those in the water?

AÇALAN.

I cannot look at them.
O cruel men! Ah! who have died to-day?
I must go hear if Tacuba was there.

SCENE II.—MEXICO.

A street of the city. Enter AZTECS, *flying, and disappear.
Enter* MUÑOZ.

MUÑOZ.

Fly, fly,—the wind my whirling sword-strokes make
Bloweth these mortal leaves out of my reach;
My legs with chasing them have all the fight.

                       Re-enter AZTECS.

Now stand, ye knaves, and give my arm a turn,
My sword a run. I have you. Ha!

    They fight; MUÑOZ *is wounded; placing his back
    to a wall, he covers his body with a shield, and
    offers at them with his sword.*

Muñoz.

                          Come on ;
Old Muñoz to a thousand of you, though
Wounded I am.

> *The* Aztecs *rush at him ; he offers at them, and*
> *they fall back.*

Muñoz.

              Though stricken to his knees,
Ye fear the old bull's horns.   Think ye I'll wait,
And tamely bleed to death?   Nay; on your spears,
And more shall keep me company.   San Pedro !

> *He runs on them, and dies fighting.*
> *Enter* Cortés *and forces.*

Cortés.

San Jago ! and at them.   Lay on !   Lay on !

> *They fight, the* Aztecs *retreat, and exeunt the*
> Spaniards *pursuing.*
>
> *Re-enter* Cortés.

Cortés, *approaching* Muñoz's *body.*

And so, at last, old Muñoz, thou art dead :
A sum of villanies most strangely mixed
With virtues ; such as joined to noble aims

Are stuff of heroes.   Aims tell on us all:
Some shoot the stars, some splinter on a stone.
He was the wordy brawler of the camp,
As vicious as a kicking horse; a gambler
And a buffoon; while sure to brave the most
Of peril, hunger, and fatigue without
Complaint, yet in the calm of plenteous ease
To fret with turbulence and yearn for treason,
There was more mischief in his idle hours
Than in the business of a thrifty knave.
Ay, treason: thou wert with Antonio
Most traitorous; ye both have served me well.
Antonio I hanged, death's warning board,
To mark a dangerous road, and thou hast fought
Bravely for me; now that account is squared.
It was shrewd work; I never did more wisely:
The rest will serve as well; better for me
They stop a breach than wastefully be hanged.

Enter ISTRISUCHIL *and* TEZCUCAN ALLIES.

ISTRISUCHIL, *to* CORTÉS.

Where are these cowards?   Must we fight with air,
And blow against the wind?   March we to blunt
Our spears like picks on walls and empty houses;
To wait while others fight, our valorous

And hungry appetites edged o'er the feast
That others surfeit of? Show us the fight,
Or home we go, and send to place us boys
To study war.

Sounds of distant strife come feebly.

CORTÉS.

Have patience; you shall fight
Enough to sweeten peace.   Dost thou not hear?
This errant breeze has wafted to our ears
The battle still is hot.

ISTRISUCHIL.

Ay, and let us blow
Its roaring flames until they lick the skies.

Enter MESSENGER.

MESSENGER.

Succor our forces, or the day is lost,
We are beset by such a multitude.
So desperate that, though we slay a man
At every stroke, we cannot drive them back;
But on our foremost files they roll, and crush
Us with their numbers.

CORTÉS.

Hark ! the battle nears.

MESSENGER.

I saw our forces last, a narrow ribbon,
That fluttered in a wind of men, they swayed
Among the enemy.

CORTÉS.

Istrisuchil,
Now on, and prove thyself a valiant man.

Exeunt all.

SCENE III.—MEXICO.

The great square of the city. GUATEMOZIN,
TACUBA, OYOT, *and* CULQUIL. *The* AZTEC
SOLDIERS *are marching by in the direction of
the battle, which is outside; the* SPANIARDS *are
striving to enter the square.*

TACUBA.

Your majesty, they are in full retreat ;
At first they drove our forces back and reached

The middle of the square; then we let loose;
All thought of life was lost in direst rage.
We pressed so closely on we could not strike,
But pushed them out; they broke, and still
      they fly.

GUATEMOZIN, *to soldiers.*

On, on to victory! Strike at their faces;
There all the senses come to learn of you,
And let the lesson be blind eyes, deaf ears,
Dumb mouths, death, death.
      The Spanish trumpets sound a charge.
        Ye falter; stand to it;
Yield not a foot of ground.

TACUBA, *to* GUATEMOZIN.
      Our impetus
Hath spent itself, we waver whether to stand
Or to be beaten back. Shall I bring up
All our reserves, and rest our fortunes on
The final struggle?

GUATEMOZIN.
      Ay; hasten, or lost
Is all we gained.
      Exit TACUBA.

GUATEMOZIN, *to soldiers.*

Soldiers, would ye be slaves?
See wives and children slaves? Turn back for love
Of earth and hope of heaven. Follow your king,
And charge them home. For Mexico strike! strike!

OYOT.

Your majesty, you must retire; the fight
Is coming near; all hope is buoyed on
Thy safety.

GUATEMOZIN.

What! do ye command your king?

CULQUIL.

To have thee king and not a bloody corse,
And all our fortunes dying in your wounds.

GUATEMOZIN.

O! that I could uncrown my head to show
These men their duty! Turn, ye cowards. O!
That Tacuba and the reserves were here!

OYOT.

Away, away.

GUATEMOZIN.

What fell and loitering
Accident stays their march?

Exeunt GUATEMOZIN, OYOT, *and* CULQUIL.

Enter the SPANISH FORCES *and* TEZCUCAN
ALLIES, *driving the* MEXICANS. ISTRISUCHIL
is fighting by the side of CORTÉS.

Exeunt MEXICANS.

CORTÉS.

Blow the recall,
We go no farther, night is in the eve;
If days were longer we could conquer now,
But wild confusion lurks about our arms
If night delays us here.

While the SPANIARDS *are forming in the square,
enter* TIZOC, OYOT, CULQUIL, *and other* MEX-
ICANS *on the roofs of houses, and renew the
fight, hurling down stones and javelins.*

CORTÉS.

Form in your ranks,
And backward move, slowly, move as one man.

OYOT, *from the house-top.*

Ye treacherous Tezcucans, we slay you,—
Our hearts have done it.   Curses, curses heap
You deeper thrice than dead men's bones entombed,
Our love will never live again.

CULQUIL.

Ingrates
With beastly hearts, breakers of pledges, deaf
To every call of honor, with ears as wide
As gates for villany to enter in,
We'll make your bodies fields to grow up spears.
A loyal fruit that all may eat and fear
Your treason.

The SPANIARDS, *having partly retreated from the
square, enter,* AZTECS *pressing after them.*

CORTÉS.

They feel us yield, and jump like springs
Against us.   Hold, hold down.   Forward, and hold
Them till our rear is clear.

The AZTECS *are driven back again.*

OYOT, *pointing.*

Look ! look ! the traitor !
Yon is Istrisuchil.

Tizoc, *calling.*

Istrisuchil,
Thou baby-man, sucker of Spanish paps,
Thy blood would soil my spear. I'll send my slaves
To slaughter thee with bills and pruning-hooks.

ISTRISUCHIL.

Ha! Prince Tizoc, high walls make naughty tongues.
Exeunt SPANIARDS *and* ALLIES; ISTRISUCHIL
shaking his spear threateningly at TIZOC.
Enter AZTECS.

SCENE IV.—MEXICO.

A street of the city.   Before a battle.

Enter CORTÉS, ALDERETE, PANFILIO, JERONIMO, PEDRO,
FERNAN, *and other soldiers.*

CORTÉS.

Against my judgment, but to yours, I yield.
This enterprise is doubly on thy care ;
The common peril and thy credit's loss
If failure comes of it.

ALDERETE.

We cannot fail.
Think of our hardships, night and day encamped
Without a shelter; our bed the miry ground;
Our tents down-pouring clouds; our food mildewed
And sour; our clothing wet like fishes' coats,
And countless small annoyances that pain;
The stinging mites, harder than greater ones
Because they will not rest.   Were we like storks
This swamp would be our home; but, being men,
We love dry ground.

SOLDIERS.

Ay; house us in the city.

CORTÉS.

Though hard, 'tis safer here; but better it,
Alderete, the causeway thou wilt take;
Be circumspect; on both its sides are deep,
Wide waters; on your flanks the enemy
Will fight in boats, and balk pursuit; have care,
And when thou find'st a breach commingling deeps
Elsewise had flowed apart, or broken bridge,—
'Tis done to stop our march,—delay thou there;
First fill the gap a safe and solid path,
Then on and win success.

ALDERETE.

Oh, never fear!
Suspicious, and with cat-like feet, we'll test
Each foot of ground.

CORTÉS.

Remember, fill each breach,
Or in the turn of battle thou art trapped.

ALDERETE.

Trust an old soldier.

CORTÉS.

I will take this street,
Converging with thine own, both centre one.
Send messages, as you advance, how goes
The battle.   We will join our forces at
The market-place.   Remember, fill each breach.

ALDERETE.

Oh, general! let us advance.

CORTÉS.

Go.

ALDERETE.

Comrades,
Onward, and ere night fall we'll dry ourselves
In Guatemozin's palace.   On ! on ! on !

> *Exeunt* ALDERETE, PANFILIO, JERONIMO, PEDRO,
> FERNAN, *and soldiers in one direction, and*
> CORTÉS *in another.*

SCENE V.—MEXICO.

Another street of the city.   A part of the same
battle.   Enter OYOT, CULQUIL, *and other*
AZTECS, *flying.*

OYOT.

Stop ! We will wait again ; when in bow-shot
Let fly at them, to prick their fury on,
And then away.

CULQUIL.

Their anger is the bait
We angle with.   The foolish fishes bite ;
We'll land them high and dry.

OYOT.

They come in shot ;
Now shoot (*they let off their arrows*).   Away, away,
they are on us !

Exeunt all.

Enter CORTÉS, FARFAN, *and soldiers pursuing.*

CORTÉS.

Come to a stand ; we gain suspiciously ;
They lure us on with seeming chance to strike,
And then are off, like frightened birds, to flit
Out of the fowler's reach.

Enter MESSENGER *from* ALDERETE.

CORTÉS, *to* MESSENGER.

How goes it with
Alderete ?

MESSENGER *hands a paper to* CORTÉS.

CORTÉS, *reading.*

We meet with no resistance ;
We have approached almost the market-place.

Alderete.

So soon ; can he have filled
The breaches in the causeway ?   And if not,

He is in jeopardy.   The clanging strife
Should reach us here.   'Tis ominously still!
Is it he blindly falls into a trap?
Farfan, advance to where yon street this joins;
Hold with your company the vantage ground:
No farther go, nor let a careless foe
Unguard your watch, or tempt you to pursuit.
Of aught amiss, send word.   I with the rest
Must take precautious care some churlish fault
May not deprive what easily were ours
By bravery.   I go to Alderete.

Exeunt CORTÉS *and a part of the soldiers.*

SCENE VI.—MEXICO.

*The broken bridge.   Another part of the same
battle. Enter* ALDERETE, PANFILIO, JERONIMO,
PEDRO, FERNAN, *and other soldiers.*

ALDERETE.

A huge, deep cut!   This will delay our march
Beyond our patience, already fretted to

8

A sweat by hinderances.   Fill up the breach ;
Tear off the stones, and hurl them in the flood.

    The soldiers work at filling the breach.

    ALDERETE, *to soldiers.*

Fill up ! fill up !   Ye work like sleepy men ;
Is there no bottom to the hole ?

    JERONIMO, *aside, to soldiers.*

        'Tis hungry
For stones as he for gold.

    ALDERETE.

       This dilatory,
And unforeseen, and most inimical pause
Breaches the solid movement of our march,
And danger floods the gap.   We must go on,
Our foes but gather strength while we stay here ;
We all can swim.   Panfilio, remain
And fill the breach, then join us with thy force.
I and the army will go forward,—breast
These waters.   Hasten in the work and share
Our glory.   Forward.

  ALDERETE *and the army cross the breach, and exeunt.*

PANFILIO.

So I am left behind
To waste my opportunities in work,
The dull background where knightly deeds are blazed,
Forgotten in their shine ; to fill a ditch
By opening betwixt my interest
And me a wider gap ; and what reward ?
To see this one's promotion, that one's honor.
The braggart action fills the world with praise,
Because the eye loves color and the ear
Loves sound.   If eyes and ears are such, need I
Do thankless work ?   Men neither see nor hear
The patient, humble, unrewarded deeds
That are the bony frame, the muscles strong,
And lungs of true renown ; but mouth and kiss
A rosy cheek, and praise the boastful cries
Of wagging tongues.   So, so ; I am no fool !

(*To the soldiers.*)

How goes the work ?

JERONIMO.

The breach is hard to fill.

PANFILIO.

The dullest hind is equal to the task
Of tumbling stones.

(*To the soldiers.*)

       Jeronimo, remain
With half my company and fill the breach;
The rest will march with me and aid our army
In the grand assault: fill up the ditch, then on,
And follow me. (*To those with him.*) Forward,
  and join our friends.

       Exeunt PANFILIO *and soldiers.*

JERONIMO.

Comrades, these stones are heavy.

PEDRO.

         Ay, the last
I heaved near broke my back.

JERONIMO, *sitting down.*

       Let's rest ourselves.
How like you, comrades, this foundation work?

PEDRO.

I like it not: 'tis not a soldier's choice.

JERONIMO.

We common soldiers are foundation stones:
Our bodies, mortared fast by discipline,

Lie hidden and forgot beneath the dome
Called glory, where no better men than we
Have lightful home.

FERNAN.

                We are the solid base
Of all; should we but shake ourselves 'twould fall.

JERONIMO.

Why do we fight?

PEDRO.

           For gold?

JERONIMO.

                There is none here.

FERNAN.

Then let us go, and get it where it is.

PEDRO.

We must fill up the breach.

JERONIMO.

             They swam it once,—
Can swim again.

PEDRO.

Cortés will punish us.

JERONIMO.

We follow good example ; surely what
Our betters leave is best for us, if aught
Goes wrong (Cortés is too precautious), but
If aught goes wrong, on them will fall his wrath.
First Alderete,—Cortés will stop there,—
He is to blame ; then on Panfilio
Will Alderete hurl small thunderbolts ;
On us Panfilio, the popinjay,
Comes with his flash in th' pan.

FERNAN.

Ay, let us go.

> *Exeunt, all crossing the breach. Enter* CORTÉS
> *and soldiers.*

CORTÉS.

'Tis as I feared.   O, fool impetuous !
To scorn delay, the slow but sure, to risk
A battle—that of all uncertain things
Most likely turns on something unforeseen—
With this worst enemy, with biting mouth

And widened throat to swallow up a host,
All hungry in thy rear.

CORTÉS, to the soldiers.

       To work, my men ;
We must fill up the breach with utmost speed.
With repetitious urgency, that trenched
Upon the wisdom which would choose to lead
An enterprise, one like a boy in mind,
Whose thoughts are full of play, and need an oft
Repeated lesson, I warned him, but in vain.
And yet we have to trust such men, and o'er
The edge of sharp necessity to hang,
Our only hold the finger strength of wits,
Which, if not reinforced, will drop us down
To ruin.

* The great* AZTEC *trumpet sounds in the distance,*
*   followed by a great shout.*

      The Aztec trumpet sounds to battle ;
That hideous yell has peopled all the air
With charging foes.   What thousands are on them,
And I not there !   O this iron—this stone—
This dungeòn of impossibility !
When action loudest cries for liberty,
And all our needs stretch out their pleading hands
To us for help, that shuts us prisoners !

Nay, grown too free am I, beyond my strength,
Stretched to tenuity !   I am with you !
I cheer you on—I fight—my noble soldiers !
The tumult nears us ; we are driven back !
Work for their lives !   Fill up, fill up the breach !

> CORTÉS *joins them, throwing in stones with his
> own hands.*

CORTES, *stopping.*

Too late,—we cannot do it !   Take your arms
And stand a solid front ; they must stop here.
Yonder they come, the tumbling driftwood, hurled
By a mortal freshet.

CORTÉS, *shouting to the retreating Spaniards.*

Stand !   By all the blows
Your swords have struck, and never failed to win
A victory, stand !   Make the dead a wall
To rally on !   Keep off, keep off the breach !

> *Enter* SPANIARDS, *flying; they jump into the water
> and struggle across the breach, followed by the*
> AZTECS, *who plunge in after them, and in boats
> attack* CORTÉS.

CORTÉS.

Cut down, cut down, and thrust the spluttering fiends
To sink and fill the damned hole !   Pull out
Our comrades !   Keep the form unbroken !   Now,
San Jago ! and at them !   Lay on ! lay on !

> *Fighting ; finally exeunt* CORTÉS *and* SPANIARDS,
> *forced back by the* AZTECS.

Enter TACUBA, OYOT, CULQUIL, *and* MAXTLA.

OYOT.

Ha ! ha ! ha ! ha !   The gods are with us now !
How we did rumple up and tear to rags
The war-wove fabric of their army's power !

MAXTLA.

Truly, they thought we were afraid of them.

CULQUIL.

We only drew our breaths to blow at them,   ·
When, dust and feathers, how we swept them out.

> *Enter* GUATEMOZIN.

TACUBA, *to* GUATEMOZIN.

My lord, we have fulfilled all your commands.

GUATEMOZIN.

A few brief words, a modest speech withal ;
But with the commentary of to-day
On them, the brightest deed in history :
Ay, one that reaches to the future for
Unwritten leaves to fully tell the story
Of to-day.   Soldiers, uncertainty is gone,
And Mexico saved.   We will go praise the gods
For what is done to-day.

SOLDIERS.

Long live the king !

Shouting and confusion of joy.

SCENE VII.—MEXICO.

A room in the palace.　Açalan *sitting at a window,
singing, the while; enter* Tacuba.

Song.

Ah, little birds beware!
　　If you dare
To sing a sweeter tune,
　　I'll ensnare
You all to love the moon,
So little birds beware.

And up, up ye will fly
　　In the sky,
And search it for my boon;
　　Would ye care
In love how high the moon!
So little birds beware.

Then down, down ye will fall,
　　Songs and all,
For flying far too high
　　In the air;
And loveless ye will die,
So little birds beware.

TACUBA.

Thou art merry, Açalan.

AÇALAN.

     Why should I not
Be happy ? Hope has turned a smiling face
Again. This dread calamity that stared
At us with horrid looks is fading off,
A vapor that took form unreal of woe.
How brightly crimsons in the west the sun ;
With what a flood he fills the room.

TACUBA.

        Oh ! ay,
The setting sun.

AÇALAN.

    And see, he spreads above,
And reaches to the east.

TACUBA.

     The dark, sad east.

AÇALAN.

No longer sad, her cheeks are blushing joy :
He kissed good-night, and said I come at morn.
I sat here singing, when, perched on a tree,

A choir of mocking-birds outrivalled me ;
And so, defiantly, I sang the song
You heard me sing.   But thou art more than gloomy.

TACUBA.

O, Mexico, thy night is coming.

AÇALAN.
                                    What
Disaster comes on us?   We conquered at
The broken bridge.   Did not the priests predict
Our foes to be destroyed, our triumph sure ?
Have not their allies fallen off like leaves
Dropped by a dying tree ?

TACUBA.
                              · All this, alas !
The time is gone, but not our foes.

AÇALAN.
                                  So soon,
And they yet here !   I was so full of joy,
The hours were winged like pretty birds that flash
Their feathers in the sun ; nay, Tacuba,
It is not gone, the gods are true.

TACUBA.

　　　　　　　　　　　　　　　The priests
Have proved themselves the liars of the gods:
The allies of our foes return to them;
They come invisibly as leaves in spring;
Each morn there is more, and darker falls the shade.
I fear the Spaniards not; we fall by hands
We taught to war, we sting ourselves to death.
Istrisuchil, your brother, led the way,
And robbed us of Tezcuco; and they go
One ally now, and now another.   States
Our arms have raised from abject slavery,
Enriched, and shielded with continual peace,
Have turned against us parricidal hands.
This city, built on islands, has no fields
To grow the fruitful maize and noble agave.
Our bread comes from our allies on the lands
That bound our lake.   If they refuse us aid,
Whence comes our food?   Already we are pinched,
A scant supply is coming from a few;
When all are gone starvation conquers us.
There's reason in my gloom, to think to see
Thee droop and fade, and shrivel up and die.

Enter TIZOC, *and listens unperceived.*

AÇALAN.

Istrisuchil! Why was he not another's,
And not my brother; kin in blood as heart
To some unmotherly one, who killed her babe
Because she wearied of him?

TACUBA.

Hatest thou

Beyond forgiveness?

AÇALAN.

Ay.

TACUBA.

I hoped when all
The evil came, and our last strength were gone,
Thou mightst a refuge find with him.

AÇALAN.

What, I?

O, any other deep of woe than that!

TACUBA.

We men make war; we are effect and cause,
And on ourselves judicially inflict

Its penalties; but ye are innocent,
And should not perish with the guilty.

AÇALAN.

No;

There is no division here, we share your joys,
May we your sorrows?   We have double grief,
And on our private pains, vain of your love,
Looking for smiles, we place these tearful gems,
Calling as doth a bride her lord to see
Of what abundant beauty is his gift.
Let us be wedded to one sorrow though
Maidenhood sparkles with the hopes of earth.

TACUBA.

Thou wilt not then make friends with him?

AÇALAN.

Wilt thou

Insult me more?   O, Tacuba, thou hast
Disgraced me in thy heart; some other love,
A low and selfish woman, formed by thee,
Deception of the mind.   Go, leave me alone;
I cannot talk to thee.

TACUBA.

Pardon, I thought

To save thee.

AÇALAN.

What ! wouldst thou intrust me to

A fiend ?

TACUBA.

Forgive——

AÇALAN.

Didst thou not hope to save

Thyself, not me ?

TACUBA.

Never.   I will not live

To see my country's ruin.

AÇALAN.

Ah, Tacuba,

I doubt thee.

Exit AÇALAN.

TACUBA.

O, was ever love so lost

Within the darkest woods of fear like mine ?

The path I found, and hoped would lead me out,

9

Ended a deeper maze; some savage beast
Made it; my folly tears my heart away.

Exit TACUBA.

TIZOC, *advancing.*

A lover's quarrel, after the approved
And ancient models.   If friends so easily
Fall out, how can our hands, when enemies,
Keep off each other's throats?   She mate with him!
No, no.   With what brave beauty strode she off!
But he lugubriously is endowed;
His face belies him not.   Our cause was ne'er
More prosperous; and were it not, I might
Be friendly with Istrisuchil, or be
The enemy of self I never was:
With Guatemozin is success.   Methinks—
Ay, ay, this quarrel 'l turn me good;
This rill, that wanders and is lost in sands,
Tapped by a trench that through my meadows runs,
To irrigate my fortunes, and at last
The spy I've played on them be well rewarded.
I must concert a plan to profit of it.

ACT IV.

SCENE I.—MEXICO.

*A street of the city, outside of the barrier. After a
battle; the dead are lying where they fell.*

> *Enter* Tizoc, *holding a scroll.*

Tizoc.

The safest is the wisest policy.
First hazard little, then, if need be, more
And more, as would a dainty thief who metes
The vessel which he fills with precious oil,
Little by little, that he spill it not,
And tell-tale waste proclaim the robbery.
The king will pass this way; he daily goes
The outposts round.   Befriend me, chance, this time;
If he once sees this scroll the thing is done.

> *Opening and reading the scroll.*

Istrisuchil, the Lord of Tezcuco,
To his ally, the Lord of Tacuba:
The ancient friendships of our thrones are joined

By durable and common interests ;
Though broken to the eye, our neighboring shores,
Beneath the quarrelling of tempests, join.
Thou art secure ; bring Açalan to me,
My messenger is trusty.

                                        If the king

Be not persuaded, Açalan will be,
That Tacuba a traitor is.

                        Approaching one of the slain.

                        Tezcucan ;

And by his badge one of the body-guard
Of Istrisuchil.   His hands grasp at the air,
While clutching at the foe in rage he died.

                Placing the scroll in the dead man's hand.

Grip that, my boy ; that stiffened arm will hold
Untiringly.   He is the instrument
Most fit to give the king the scroll : he 'll look
That whilst 'twas carried to Lord Tacuba
To 've been smote down ; so violently stopped
The life in him, that death with rigor kept
This attitude, and holding up the scroll
He lies, and shows how he was carrying it.
Then comes the king, and sees it ; some disclosure
Of Cortés' plans, he thinks, is to be found ;
When, lo ! 'tis Tacuba a traitor is.

Within this broken dwelling I will ensconce
Myself, and watch the end ; and none too soon.

                              TIZOC *hides.*

Enter GUATEMOZIN *and* TACUBA.

GUATEMOZIN.

O, Tacuba ! this swift, resistless blast
We fly against ; we rise and beat the air,
Are stationary,—then no weary bird
Flies with the storm, driven by springing winds,
More rapidly than we, on, on to pierce
The thick'ning troubles madly striven from.

TACUBA.

When once the current turns, or destiny
Reaches a hand remorseless, large, and strong
Enough to grasp a star, and crack its shell
As easily as thou or I an egg ;
Reaches and takes us 'tween the thumb and finger,
Ah, what are we ?   We crumble in the hand,
As butterflies leave on our fingers dust,
Go lame and die, killed by the lightest touch.

GUATEMOZIN.

But we must struggle on, and foot by foot
Contest the ground ; 'twere cowardice, default

Of duty, not.   Futurity, who knows :
Though every finger of adversity
Spread like converging rays from lurid fires,
That burn unseen beneath the verge of vision,
Though they brighten while we weary at the work,
We must not leave the labor of to-day.

TACUBA.

If we must perish, and I feel we will,
It will be utterly; then why bear we
Labor and pain for naught?   Let us sit down
Until insensible, still as the hills,
We turn to dust, and leave our history
A web that stretches out unwoven threads
Over the future, struck by deathless winds,
That sweep the hollows of eternity,
To quiver, and complain on ears forever.

GUATEMOZIN.

The law of life is live as if forever,
The present always is, the future never.
It is the voice of faithful nature; she
Surrenders not, knows no captivity;
The plant sends down its roots and up its leaves
For sustenance.   The parching drought may come,

It searches for, drinks the last drop, and dies;
It does not turn a bird, and fly away.

> *They approach the dead* TEZCUCAN, TIZOC *from
> his hiding place eagerly watching them, when
> enter a company of starving* AZTECS *searching
> for food.   A* WOMAN *finds on one of the slain
> some food, a man snatches it from her, and·
> runs away.*

WOMAN, *running after him.*

'Tis mine, 'tis mine; O, mercy, give it me!

> *Exeunt* MAN *and* WOMAN.

> *This engages the attention of* GUATEMOZIN *and*
> TACUBA; *they pass without seeing the scroll.*

GUATEMOZIN.

This last recourse to search the dead for food!
Ah, Tacuba, my starving people; woe
Is me,—I have no food.   To-day I watched
A warrior while here the battle raged,
He fought so bravely; near him stayed his wife,
As near as would the press of battle grant;
She held her babe, and covered with a shield
Dropped by some fallen soldier; when the strife

Allowed she bore her husband arrows, gave
Them with a kiss.   I marvelled at such love.
And when the soldier fell, she ran to him,
She kissed his lips, and strove to stanch his wound ;
But vainly, which she knew, and stopped and gazed,
Her dry and parched cheeks unmoistened by
A healing tear, gazed on the wasting bloom
That plashed upon the ground, now on her child ;
And then her face with such commingled love
And horror shown, and to his bleeding breast
She placed the starving child, and let it suck ;
Which, when his father knew, he turned,
Looked on his wife.   It was immortal ; there
Was something more than human in his face ;
It said my life is freely given,—live, my child.
And then it dimmed, as doth the polished gold
Grow dull when breathed upon, and he was dead.

TACUBA.

And yet such valor, such devotion fails
To save us.

GUATEMOZIN.

Knowest thou the future ?

Exeunt GUATEMOZIN *and* TACUBA.

TIZOC *emerges from concealment.*

Tizoc.

                              Faugh !
Unkingly nonsense.   What have we to do,
Whose veins are filled with rarest blood of earth,
With common griefs?   The common die for us ;
We live for self.

Taking the scroll away.

I'll stake my life on't next.

SCENE II.—MEXICO.

Inside the barrier.

Oyot, Culquil, Maxtla, *and others.   A tumult; the*
people running together.

A Voice.

Give up the city.

Maxtla.

                    Ay, let us surrender ;
We are unfit to fight more.

OYOT.

     No ; we'll fight ;
Better to die a freeman than a slave !
Cry down the cowards !   We will fight !

VOICES.

     Fight ! fight !

MAXTLA.

Cowards ! our bravery, has it not shown ?
Ye all know me ; mine own familiar friend
Might not for this disguise of wounds and what
'This pilfering famine leaves me—skin and bones.
Cowards ! when brave men find the battle gone,
Are they bereft of reason, such as fear
Deprives the mind, that they must blindly rush
On certain doom ?   Let us surrender now ;
The time our wounds are healed we will renew
The war ; we perish uselessly elsewise.

FIRST AZTEC.

Ay, we will fight no more.

SECOND AZTEC.

     Fight ! do ye call
This fighting, barely strong enough to lift

Our swords?   We strike so lightly, they no more
Ward off our blows.

FIRST AZTEC.

Our final overthrow,
Because we are so numerous, delays ;
They weary killing us.

THIRD AZTEC.

If we had food,
We would fight.

FOURTH AZTEC.

I broke my fast this morn on slime
I scraped from off the buttress of the bridge ;
It had a watery, mildewy taste,
But I feel stronger for 't, and am for war.

FIFTH AZTEC.

I ate a toad.

FIRST AZTEC.

There's poison in its head.

FIFTH AZTEC.

I ate it head and all, and I say fight.   (*Retorting.*)
And what hadst thou to eat?   Thou shudderest.

FIRST AZTEC.

No matter what; I had enough.

FIFTH AZTEC.

                          Enough?

Thou lucky man!

FOURTH AZTEC.

                  He means more than enough.
How pale he gets? He sickens on it.

A WOMAN, *one demented by suffering.*

                         Eat, eat;
With eating teeth are worn away.   See, mine
Are precious pearls,—for so my lover said;
I will not harm with eating what he praised.
How sweetly sing the birds—

> Cheerily, cheerily, blithely and free,
> Not any, not any sorrow have we;
> Up with the breezes, we flutter away,
> Down by the roses to swing on a spray.
>
> Merrily, merrily, dwell we the trees,
> Twittering, snapping the goldenest bees;
> Singing of summer, and loving begun,
> Warm as a lily abloom in the sun.

And they eat worms,
And worms eat men.   How fat they are, and we
So lean, so lean.   Ha! ha! ha!   (*Showing her teeth.*)
Don't they glisten?
He said they did.   Saw ye him?

OYOT.
She is crazed.

THE WOMAN.

He went to battle now two days agone;
Hungry,—he starved himself for me,—and I
Shall never eat again.   Ah, me! no more.

OYOT.

Good woman, thy lover is dead.

THE WOMAN.
Dead, dead?
Dead, dead?   No, no!   No, no!   He is alive!
No, I am dead; come to my funeral;
There'll be fine cakes and drink for you.

She wanders to one side.

MAXTLA.
On eating
Always.   Poor thing!   The agony which fills
This city, were it substance, 'twould be hard,

And arch us o'er in such a stony cell
That mercy, though it grasp the thunderbolts
Of all the upper skies, and hurl them on't,
It would not break.   Our every hope is gone!

WOMAN, *returning.*

I found his shield and spear, and a dead man;
I buried him.

> Flowers for the head,
> Flowers when we wed,
> Flowers for the dead.

Flowers are beautiful;
They are not hungry; they eat dirt—there's plenty:
Dead men are turned to dirt.   The birds eat worms,
And worms eat men; so do the flowers sweet:
His lips make pinks—there's honey; out o' his cheeks
Come roses; violets make eyes for some,
For him are pansies, gold and dark; and lilies
Bloom in his teeth, and grasses in his hair.
Did ye see him?   Tell him to come to me.
Give me some bread.   (*Begging, and they refusing.*)
Thou, sir.   Thou, sir.   Ah, me!
Exit woman.

MAXTLA.

Good citizens, yield to the general wish.

CULQUIL.

Be not deceived ; if we had yielded while
Our city stood, we would have homes ; save these,
All is a ruin !　What is life without
Companionship?　Are not our friends, our wives,
And children dead?　Then let us die, and die
Not by the slow and base decease of slaves,
Of all our ancient enemies the scorn,
To see the treachery of friends rewarded
With parting of our power ; let us live
But for one purpose, to revenge our wrongs,
And die with joy of battle in our hearts.

OYOT.

Ay, let us die like men accepting death,
Not fleeing with our eyes distent by fear
To see the deeper depths of trouble, nor
With eyes bedimmed, blinded with grief, to what
The conqueror looks whom we beseech, contempt,
Granting our prayers with our slavery ; but
With eyes calm as the lake that ruffles not,
When all the blood of dying day is shed,
And calmer grows as darker falls the night.
Have not our hearts o'er olden stories burned
Of how our fathers died ?
Now, we may die as gloriously.

VOICES.

No surrender !   Let
Us go defy the enemy !

Enter TACUBA.

OYOT.

Here comes
The Lord of Tacuba. (*Accosting him.*) Has Cortés sent
Ambassadors to treat for our surrender?

TACUBA.

Ay.

OYOT.

What has willed the king?

TACUBA.

He, moved by pity,
Seeing your sufferings, has closed his heart
To what his valor willed, and is resolved
To yield the city.

OYOT.

Never ! he shall not !
We want no pity.   Go to him and plead
For us, most noble Tacuba, that he
Dishonor not his reign, or make us shame.

Enter AMBASSADORS, *going to* CORTÉS.

Oyot.

Bear ye the terms surrendering the city?

Ambassador.

In the king's name, let us pass.

Oyot.

           Come all, and stop

This shame.

Oyot, *to the* Ambassadors.

    Back to the king, and tell him we,
The people, have refused to let you go.

Ambassador.

You are disloyal.

Oyot.

     Nay, we have no king.
He has dethroned himself, surrendered us,
And now we owe allegiance to ourselves.
We vote for war.

Ambassador.

     He will be very wroth,
And punish you.

OYOT.

  With arson? Doth a man,
Whose house incendiary flames enwrap,
To put them out build fires within? What pains
Of punishment are greater than we bear?
Would he add slavery?
        Enter GUATEMOZIN.

GUATEMOZIN, *to* AMBASSADORS.

  Why stand ye here?

AMBASSADOR.

The populace have set themselves against
Our going.

GUATEMOZIN.

  Let them pass, good citizens.

A VOICE.

No, no! Hast thou forgot King Montezuma?
We slew him for no worse a thing than this
Thou doest.

GUATEMOZIN.

  Shame on you; is it, base churls,
For this that I have clouded manliness
With shadows of your woe! 'Tis easy when

We suffer injury to loose our wrath.
There is relief and riotous joy in vengeance;
But to forego, to still the tempest down
That rages in the heart, by freezing o'er
A righteous anger; to congeal the warm
And noble passions of our being, lest
If they should reign ye would be sufferers,
Is harder.   Had I yielded to my heart
Its dearest wish, I would have dared the worst
That could befall a mortal man ere I
Surrendered.

CULQUIL.

          He is our king, our noble king;
We yield all to thy will.

OYOT.

                         Pity us not;
Or, if thou pitiest, hear us, O king.
Pity the rage that fills our bosoms, seen
The desolation fallen on our homes;
Our kindred, all that made life lovable, gone
Forever; we would join their company,
And come to them smiling the light of battle;
Not cringing as base slaves, who change the lash
Their master scourges with for conscience' whip.

GUATEMOZIN.

Have ye your will.   The need for treaty is gone.

Exeunt GUATEMOZIN, TACUBA, *and* AMBASSADORS.

CULQUIL.

Hasten, and man the ramparts.

FIRST AZTEC.

Ay, we come ;
We are decrepit with hunger ; grown old.

SECOND AZTEC.

Look up, what loathsome clouds will rain on us ;
Yon vultures circle o'er our heads.

THIRD AZTEC.

A sign !
A sign ! behold with them an eagle flies.

MAXTLA.

The end is near: this morn, when rose the priests
To daily sacrifice, a serpent coiled,
And hissed upon the altar.

FIRST AZTEC.

What doth this mean ?

MAXTLA.

Hast thou forgotten of our cognizance
Of state? An eagle clutching in his claws
A writhing snake; the eagle's flown up there,
The serpent's here.

FIRST AZTEC.

　　　　　Why do we fight? Let us
Lie down and die.

MAXTLA.

　　　　　Last night I saw above
The lake, which looked all blood, a bandage bind
The firmament, from which dropped crimson fire,
As if the heavens were wounded.

OYOT.

　　　　　Signs and signs;
No better signs than we are to ourselves.

FIRST AZTEC.

Listen, I hear the steady march of forces:
Let us go down, 'tis weariness to fight;
We will lie down and die. (*Descending.*)

　　　　　　　　Enter AÇALAN

Açalan.

The enemy !

Do ye desert your posts ?

Maxtla.

We cannot fight ;

'Tis useless.

Açalan.

What ! a woman weak as I
Show men their duty. I will call your wives,
And we will watch the walls, and ye may go.
No, ye are brave ; the gods will pity us :
A breath to nerve the winds they need but give
To blow our foes like broken straws away.

First Aztec.

I feel a sudden quickening of air,
As if a god had turned and looked on us.

The wind rises.

The wind ! the wind !

Oyot.

Let us return to duty.

They man the ramparts again.

AÇALAN.

To be a woman is to yield to man.
When clanging arms and battle cries are loud :
The time for argument is gone : love is dethroned,
She, Queen of Reason, sits a lonesome one,
Tear-dimmed, with all her courtiers gone.   Could I
But plead with them to go away and leave
Us to our own the happiness and peace
Which culprits are, by not an act of ours,
Of wrong the Spaniards have, they would not heed
My gentle glances or soft words, could I
Look tenderly on monsters such as these ?
No ; we must stand and see our brothers fight.
Why were we not endowed with strength and armed,
That love might reign in battle for the right ?

OYOT.

The enemy are coming on us !   Up !
Up, and at them !

> *Trumpets are heard outside sounding a charge,
> and* SPANIARDS *heard shouting and rushing to
> the attack.   The* AZTECS *defy and hurl their
> javelins down on them.*

COLQUIL.

        Come on our thorny bush ;
'Tis dry and stubborn.

OYOT, *drawing his bow.*

        Fly, my arrow ; peck
Yon boaster in the eye.

MAXTLA.

        Come up, come up
To us. Why tarry you ? Come to our eyrie ;
Ha ! ha ! we are too rough for these gay birds.

AÇALAN, *ascending the rampart.*

Give me a spear, I'll strike one loyal blow
For Mexico.

    *She takes a spear from a soldier and hurls it
      down, then turns and covers her face.*

OYOT.

They fly ! The gods are with us !

        The conflict ceases.

AÇALAN, *descending.*

He looked at me ; his fair and youthful face
Had pity in it. Did I slay him ?

MAXTLA.

Nay;
Thy spear smote on his casque; the summer rain
Could patter harder.

AÇALAN.

I repented it:
Weak heart, weak arm, you are well joined in me.

OYOT.

They come again.   Strike!   Strike for Mexico!

> *The* SPANIARDS *return and attack with redoubled*
> *vigor; they break down the barrier and enter.*
> *A* TEZCUCAN *seizes* AÇALAN, *and is about to*
> *slay her, when enter* ISTRISUCHIL, FARFAN, *and*
> PANFILIO.

ISTRISUCHIL, *rescuing her.*

Hold! hold! hold off! she is my sister.   Fair
Sister, 'tis many days since we have met.

AÇALAN.

Istrisuchil, thou art no more my brother;
I will not take my life from thee—slay me.

What! shall the hand that has his country slain
Be my savior, and I, by gratitude
Condoning, be accessor to the crime?
If there are men among you who have hearts
Where pity lingers yet awhile, slay me,
And rid me of this shame.

FERNAN, *to* PANFILIO.
                              As fair a woman
As ever met my eyes.   Mark how she queens
It o'er her brutish brother.

PANFILIO.
                              They are unlike
As is a lily to a toad.

ISTRISUCHIL, *seizing her.*
                              Thou wilt
Not take thy life from me!

FARFAN, *interfering.*
                              My lord, forego;
We have our general's orders to preserve
All prisoners, and those who do not fight,
From harm.   Give o'er,—dost thou persist?   Unhand

The woman, or wert thou fourfold the king
Thou art, still I would cleave thee to the weasand.

Enter an AZTEC *soldier, running.*

SOLDIER.

The king, the king is taken!   All is lost!

AÇALAN.

O, Guatemozin taken!   Lost! lost! lost!

AÇALAN *swoons.*

ACT V.

SCENE I.—MEXICO.

A room of the palace.

GUATEMOZIN *sitting with his face covered by his mantle; the* QUEEN *is regarding him sorrowfully.*

Enter AÇALAN.

THE QUEEN, *to* AÇALAN, *and pointing to* GUATEMOZIN.

See, there—he sits above companionship
In sorrow as he was in majesty.
O, Açalan, I wedded but his half,
His gentle, tender half that took delight
In me, my dalliance of wifely love,
And gave me sympathy ; that other half
He wore a crown, thought wrinkled on his brow,
And sternness closed his lips, and in his eyes
A nation looked at me, and I, abashed,
Drew back. I fear the glance of many eyes.
At times when we in thought were closest drawn
Each to the other, then has come this king,
So grand, and cold, and wise, between us.

AÇALAN.

And
Thou canst not comfort him?

QUEEN.

I cannot; he
Is more the king without his crown than when
In visible and royal state he ruled.
Wilt thou not speak to him? I have beheld
In thee the same o'ermastering that loads
My tongue with silence; thou canst find and touch
Some hidden, frozen spring to warmth again.

AÇALAN.

There is a privacy of grief, of closed
And darkened windows; dare I enter where
The light may not? A pallid modesty
Of woe, the soul disrobed of every joy,
Stands fearing his own eyes.

QUEEN.

But speak to him.
His outward stillness is the icy crust
Of coming death; it thicker grows as die
The fires hope kindles.

AÇALAN.

I will speak to him.

AÇALAN, *to* GUATEMOZIN.

O, king, awake.   He heedeth not.

QUEEN.

Again,

And louder.

AÇALAN.

O, king, awake.

GUATEMOZIN, *uncovering his face.*

Awake ! would I
Could sleep ; 'tis time to sleep.   I close my eyes,
They open inward to a larger world.
O, earth, thou art a gleaming flake that melts
Into the night, and thou, poor sun, wouldst come
To lighten me, as thou didst swaddle with
Thy beams an infant world, too monstrous grown,
Too black is this.   What cries of dying men
In echoes louder, louder coming back.
Anguish, as if all they that ever died
Were dying o'er again in my mad ears !

My eyes are hot with blood.   O, I would sleep
A dreamless sleep.   To wake is to dream.   O, what
A foolish dream was mine; I thought that courage,
Self-sacrifice, the fullest duty done,
Ay, more than done, to supplement weak hearts
And minds out of my strength, would win of gods
And men the victory.   I dreamed, I dreamed;
'Tis time to sleep, to sleep.

> *He covers his face again.*

QUEEN.

                    He will go mad,
Or die; he must be roused, some passion moved
To rush swift on his heart, and startle him;
Since love has failed, arouse his anger, let
Hate chafe the broken heart.

AÇALAN.

                    No common hurt
Will move him.

QUEEN.

         Mock, deride his sorrow; sing
Of our former greatness, sing the pæan King
Cihaupan sang bringing his captives home.

AÇALAN.

It is a song of triumph, full of pride,
Elation, and of victory; no, no;
'Tis far removed from him, as heaven from earth.
How can I sing with such a tremor in
My throat, and such a load upon my heart,
And such a song, discordant as a laugh
In th' chamber of death?

QUEEN.

If it stirs thee so,
It will move him the more.

AÇALAN.

I'll try to sing.

She sings.

I come the lord of men and kings,
A sun among the stars,
A light no lightning scars;
As tempests waste with stormy wings,
I sweep the earth with wars.

GUATEMOZIN *uncovers his face, and gazes at her.*

O, soul, thou treadest down the grass
Of nations; down they kneel,
And bow with all their weal;
They bow down to the ground and pass
Forever 'neath thy heel.

My queen looks from her window : deck
Thyself with feathers gay;
I bring thee spoil to-day,
Fine needlework meet for thy neck,
And damsels for thy prey.

GUATEMOZIN.

What ! has my reason gone, my ears turned liars,
My eyes deceivers, and my memory
Broken, its fragments patch so wrongly ?   Go !
Thou hast the voice and form of Açalan,
But she would never mock her country's fall.
O, bitter, bitter woe, that stops not at
The actual infliction, but must arm
Imagination with illusions that
Entangle good with evil, till the good
Is traitorous, and those we love unworthy.

AÇALAN.

My lord, I am Açalan.

GUATEMOZIN.

Thou substance real ?
Come near (*touching her*).   Away, I loath thee; O,
my gods,

11

Was this last blow wanting? (*To* Açalan.) Thou
    wisely waited
Until calamity had opened wounds
To strike thy dove feet in and tear me. Go!
What fools we are to let the thrifty grown,
But short-lived entities of earth, to grip
The solid trunk of us that must endure
Long after they are dead.

AçALAN.

           Thou art unjust;
When thou wert king, and strong, and bold, and fortune
Smiled on thee, what was courage but content;
Deceitful calm of seas, an accident:
For cowards may be brave when prosperous;
The substance is in us; the merit is
When all that we have wrought about our lives
To feast the ears and eyes; to yield the mind
The worthy use of thought; to prompt the soul
To noble deeds, goes as the changing year,
And nothing leaves but winter in the heart,
To stand alone thy inner fibres strong
Till summer 'turns.

GUATEMOZIN.

           Am I a brute, to crop
The herbage of content in times like these,

When every feeling weeps not for myself,
But for a glory gone ; a race extinct ;
A purpose unfulfilled ; a void, that down
Through endless ages questions of the gods
With e'er recurrence, and no answer given ?

AÇALAN.

The gods weep not.

GUATEMOZIN.

They have no cause.   Am I
A god ?

AÇALAN.

Thou art no god, alas !   I thought
Thee nearly one.   The gods are merciful ;
But weep not.

GUATEMOZIN.

It would be unnatural not ;
Betray a nature base.

AÇALAN.

I would not have
You so ; but tears are not so excellent,
That they can enter heaven.   Arouse, O king,
And sorrow like a man who yet has strength
To bear a greater burden.

GUATEMOZIN.

Am I weak,

Or has my sorrow grown presumptuous,
Usurping not mine own? But thou art strong,
Or cold: how couldst thou sing that mocking song?

AÇALAN.

Am I not used to suffering? This poor,
Sick head of mine so beaten, buffeted
By mine own sorrows, that the pains they quicken
Lie in the sense all stunned; the shooting pang
Is gone, wild agony is o'er; the dull,
Cold ache remains. Now, since the hopes I built
On thee are gone—no cure, no restitution
Possible—I grieve not; the sense is dulled.
Tears, tears have been my food. Ay, I am cold.
Rememb'rest thou a traveller, returned
From journeying the barbarous North, told thee
How that a rude and hardy people dwelt
Within the woods, and who, when brought to die,
Sung of their victories, and died with words
Of triumph on their lips?

GUATEMOZIN.

I have been weak,

Fair cousin; pardon my too angry words.

QUEEN.

O, Guatemozin, hast thou no word for me ;
Am I henceforth a houseless wanderer ;
And did thy love go with thy crown ?

GUATEMOZIN, *reaching out his arms to her.*
                                        My wife !

SCENE II.—MEXICO.

A street of the city.

Enter JERONIMO, PEDRO, FERNAN, *and* SOLDIERS.

FERNAN.

What think ye, comrades, of our spoil of wounds?
There are enough of us to stock with beggars
Three kingdoms.

JERONIMO.

                    Ay, we all are beggars to
Old miser fortune, and, like poor men's coats,
Our bodies are all over patches, rents
Sewed up, a hundred wounds : they are our coats
Of arms.

FERNAN.

Poor coats to keep out cold.

JERONIMO.

But good
Enough to show in th' wind. There's money in't;
More than is got by fighting. We will home;
(*Mimicking.*) Go begging, hat in hand,—"Good
citizens,
Your honor, may it please your worship, give
To the poor soldier wounded in the wars
A little to keep life in his old body.
Thanks; may the saints heap blessings on your head."
Foh! foh! it maddens me to think of it.

FERNAN.

Ho! ho! it makes me laugh; we are a joke,—
A fat and saucy joke in our lean eyes.
Our sober earnestness is farcical:
We have stern faces, thinned by hardships, scarred
By wounds; but back above them in the skull,
That firmament of night, what pigmies dwell
Our peopled brains, with less of sense than maggots;
They prove the cheese is rich; we that we know
How to starve.

JERONIMO.

      Comrades, truly we are fools:
Having the power, yet yielding Cortés all
To enrich himself, and we get nothing.

PEDRO.

                     Do
You think that we are cheated of our shares?

JERONIMO.

Ay, I think so; 'tis common talk. Go, read
Thou the lampoon we nailed upon his door:
One-fifth as leader and one-fifth as king,
Thou hast a thief's and traitor's reckoning.

FERNAN.

Pedro, mark me, Antonio was 'fore
His time; the army for revolt is ripe;
We'll plunder Cortés of the stolen gold.

PEDRO.

But Guatemozin said there was no gold.

JERONIMO.

Hast thou not marked of Cortes' tenderness
For this king? Trust me, he buys immunity.

Here comes the royal treasurer ; we'll lay
Our grievance and the emperor's 'fore him.

Enter ALDERETE.

Sir Alderete, thou art charged to see
The royal fifth, when we divide the spoil,
Be not diminished of an honest part.
'Tis said that Cortés treasure has concealed,
Which was uncounted when we made division ;
And that the crown is mulcted of its dues,
And we reduced to beggary.

ALDERETE.

What grounds

Have ye for such a charge?

JERONIMO.

There is a prince
Among the prisoners who, when we charged
On Guatemozin and that lord they style
Of Tacuba that they had hid the gold,
Came privately to me, and said he knew
The treasure hidden, but not where.   This, when
We told to Cortés, was not listened to ;
But he commands the def'rence due to kings
Be paid to them, and such the state they keep,

We being victors are the victims made
Of him we conquered.   This most unnatural,
Unheard of course must have some motive; none
More probable than Cortés is a gainer.

ALDERETE.

And yet a probability is at best
A shadow which we see; the substance real
May differ from the form which we imagine.
As men have shadows much alike—some lights
Make most a likeness—this may lie to us.

JERONIMO.

If Cortés is too high, is Guatemozin?
Let us demand that he be tortured; which,
If Cortés dare refuse, we will cry out
Of his complicity in what he fears
That Guatemozin will betray of him.

ALDERETE.

'Twill force him to consent; and once we have
The king upon the rack or toasting in the fire,
We'll have the truth.

ALL.

'Tis good.

ALDERETE.

                I will to Cortés,
And move him to our wishes. If he yields,
All's well; if not, we meet again and force
Him to it.

JERONIMO.

        Ay; there speaks a man; we'll wait
Thee here.

ALDERETE.

        Nay; follow me, and clamor at
His door; 'twill help my argument.

ALL.

                We will.

ALDERETE.

See yonder: he is coming here; retire,
I will accost him; watch my movements well:
I'll raise my hand for signal, then draw near
And help me: we must capture him by storm.
                Exeunt all but ALDERETE.

ALDERETE.

First, I will ply my arguments to blow
Red hot his temper; then I'll call my hammers,
And we will forge him to our purpose tight,

As iron welds with iron ; it must look
Unpreconcerted : I will caution them.

Exit ALDERETE.
Enter CORTÉS.

CORTÉS.

And now the work to do : the roofing o'er
The edifice of our conquest, which remains
To make it habitable, must be had
At dizzy heights, and half my powers lost.
A builder on the lofty walls he rears
Has narrow scope, though wider vision ; ay,
He sees how high he is, how far the fall,
And wary on the narrow ridge he clings,
One hand for labor, and one hand to hold.
Here is the madness of my soldiers wild
To peril me.   The vertigo of success
Swims in their heads, threatens authority :
They band about the city, blowing hot
And roaring like a furnace, till their fury
Scorches the prime of discipline.   Fools ! fools !
And foremost 'mong these malcontents are those
Conspirators whose head grown to the wind
Of power was blown away ; their lives are mine,
As was Antonio's.   I must forearm ;
Hither Sir Alderete, the treasurer, comes.

Re-enter ALDERETE.

CORTÉS.

Sir Alderete, what errand leads thee here
What meaning has thy quick presaging manner?

ALDERETE.

To plead the cause of men whose fortunes are
In debt to wounds they got in serving thee:
We want a fair division of the spoil.

CORTÉS.

Ye have had it.

ALDERETE.

                 But Guatemozin hides
Away so much, our share is like the dust
Of empty bins, betraying what was there
And what we lose.   Yield him to us to torture;
We'll force the truth.

CORTÉS.

            We promised otherwise.
No! no! a breach of faith a pardon finds
In no emergency.

ALDERETE, *signalling.*

                If there is gold,
He first broke faith with thee; I beg thee, thwart

Us not of this.   We feel that we are wronged:
One of the royal house of Mexico
Has vouched the hidden gold; justly incensed,
We ask to try our only way to find it;
And rumor says—and pardon if I cause
Thy ears to burn, 'tis done of friendliness—
Thou'rt party to the wrong.   Give o'er to us
The fallen king to torture; save thy name
From all complicity.

Enter SOLDIERS.

                              Thy hold upon
These soldiers is o' the past; the term of their
Enlistment was the conquest of this land;
The day of settlement is here.   The gold
Thou canst not pay with promises—the gold
Is ours already.   Yield the king to us.

CORTÉS.

Sir Alderete, truly I did think
This city full of gold, and all there was
Is fairly counted.   Charge no shame on me;
Rather would I ye had my portion all,
Could I with honor give, and pay my debts;
But ask not this.

SOLDIERS.

Justice!   Give us our gold!
Yield Guatemozin to be tortured.   Gold!
Gold! gold!   We will melt out of him the ore.

CORTÉS.

This cannot be.

A VOICE.

Art thou in league with him?

CORTÉS.

Whose voice was that? Stand forth and hear my answer;
'Twill please him less than does his question me.
No! no! no! no!   Stand back (*drawing his sword*).
Ho, guards! attend
Me here.

ALDERETE, *to soldiers.*

Fools! fools!   Away until his choler
Cools.   *Exeunt* SOLDIERS.

ALDERETE.

Still hear me, my general; thou hast foes
At court so weighty clinging to this handle,

They'll pull thee down. Velasquez burns to be
Revenged on thee; Fonseca is thy foe;
And there are always jealous ones to drag
The prosperous in the mire.

CORTÉS.

                     The balance swings:
The times, indeed, are critical with me:
Fonseca, jealous for his power, sets
Authority against our good, because
His priestly will may not say come and go,
Do this, not that, as freaky as the wind
None know the course of. I have much to fear:
This obdurate and sullen fool may gain
The emperor's ear; and now the conquest o'er,
Some fat and lazy courtier may be deemed
Sufficient for these mellow times of peace.
My safety was our danger; now I've pulled
The chestnuts from the fire. I must look to 't.

ALDERETE.

Lose not thy friends; they clamor for their rights:
Almost a mutiny now threatens thee;
Thy army is thy strength.

CORTÉS.

　　　　　　　I yield ; have ye
Your will ; but, Alderete, thou must have
Full charge, and no unneedful cruelty.

ALDERETE.

I will obey thee.

CORTÉS.

　　　　　　　Go ; leave me alone.
　　　　　　　　　Exit ALDERETE.
In spite of all, my heart misgives again ;
'Twill dim the past and make our labors more.

————

SCENE III.—MEXICO.

A room in the palace. GUATEMOZIN *and* TACUBA.

GUATEMOZIN.

Gold ! gold ! gold ! gold !　I think of it, there comes
A barrier impervious to me,

A thickening to dull, and moveless form
Of airy particles that danced my brain,
Each shining with its modicum of truth,
Like flashing motes, the sunbeam's little worlds.
What is this famine of the heart for gold?
What food to feed on !

TACUBA.

                    Strange as is their speech,
'Tis stranger.   In their land beyond the seas
I've heard it has some use to us unknown ;
The person that possesses it may have
The richest viands, costliest apparel,
House like a king's ; that men will bow, enslave
Themselves to him for it ; that it does more
Under the heavens than any other thing :
Turning men's love to hate, their hate to love ;
It conquers armies, rules great states, at last
Ruins them all ; they say that there are men
Willing to sell their country, wives, and children
For this insensible, untoothsome, cold,
But glist'ning ore.   These foreigners for gold
Have dared th' invincible, and proved it false :
O, fallen Mexico, it conquered thee.

GUATEMOZIN.

Ay, it is true : first Cortés comes and bids
Me give him gold : I said I have no more.
What disappointment flashed his cloudy face ;
A king might lose a province with less gloom.
Then Alderete, he of nimble legs,
We trapped behind the broken bridge, and cried
Gold ! gold ! and last a herd of common men
Came, all for gold, and threatened me with death.

> *Enter* ALDERETE, FARFAN, *and* SOLDIERS *bring-
> ing in two wooden settles, and two pans full of
> live coals.*

ALDERETE, *to* SOLDIERS, *and pointing at the prisoners.*

Seize and securely bind them on the seats.

> *The* SOLDIERS *seize and bind* GUATEMOZIN *and*
> TACUBA.

·ALDERETE, *to* SOLDIERS.

Place at their feet the fires.   Stay, not too near ;
Gently at first.

> *They place the fires, purposing to burn their feet.*

GUATEMOZIN.

                    What strange indignity !
Wherein have we unhaply angered you ?

ALDERETE.

I have been learning oratory, my lord;
My blunt and soldier tongue could not persuade,
So I have garnished me with certain forms
Of metaphors, the rhetoric of fire,
Which, schoolmen say, is always eloquent.
(*Pointing to the fires.*) Look you, they are brimful of
  argument.

GUATEMOZIN.

Art thou to torture me?

ALDERETE.

       Ay; or the truth.
Where is thy gold?

GUATEMOZIN.

  Ye have it.

ALDERETE, *to* SOLDIERS.

  Nearer.
    They push the fires nearer.

ALDERETE, *to the prisoners.*

       There—
With what seductive fervor it appeals.

GUATEMOZIN.

Thou fool, is lying so a part of thee?
Why should we hide the gold, who never knew
Its value till this hour?

ALDERETE.

Art thou so dull?
It is a witty flame. (*To* SOLDIERS.) Move up the fires.
The fires are pushed still nearer.
Enter AÇALAN *and the* QUEEN.

QUEEN.

What do they here? What fearful looks they have!

AÇALAN.

What weights the air with horror? It is fire!

QUEEN.

Where, where?

AÇALAN, *pointing.*

There! O, my king! O, Tacuba!
Up! up! ye burn!

QUEEN.

O, my husband !   (*She swoons.*)

AÇALAN.

I will save

You.

She runs to draw the fires away, when ALDERETE
interferes and stops her.

ALDERETE, *to* AÇALAN.

Nay, fair lady, they have chosen this.

To SOLDIERS.

Move back the fires, and let their bodies cool ;
The flames will freshen and bite harder for it.

The fires are moved back.

ALDERETE, *to* AÇALAN.

My lady, they withhold great treasure which
The general surrender gave to us ;
Bid them reveal their hidden store of gold ;
We have no other power than pain o'er them.
If they disclose, these fires shall harm no more ;
If not, they both shall toast till black as coals.

To the SOLDIERS, *and pointing to the* QUEEN.

Away with that sick woman 'fore she wakes.

The QUEEN *is carried out.*

Açalan.

My king! O, Tacuba! where is the treasure?

Tacuba.

There is none.

Guatemozin.

      Açalan, go thou to the queen,
That she have needful tendance in her troubles.

Alderete.

To work! we'll play no more.   Push up the fires
Close to their smoking heels; hot! hot as hell!

Açalan.

O, mercy! mercy!   Have you none?   You have,
Or you would be inhuman.   Sir, kind sir,
I see a gentleness that contradicts
The fearful import of your words; be moved,—
I know the king and Tacuba,—be moved;
They speak the truth; there is no gold.

Alderete.

                        No gold?

Art sure of that?

AÇALAN.

Thou art relenting; for
The love thou'lt need and find when helpless, yield;
Have mercy on these hapless prisoners.

FARFAN.

Sir Alderete, this has gone as far
As any need.

SOLDIERS.

Ay, ay; they have no gold,
Is plain enough.

TACUBA.

Why was I left to live?
O! O! O! O! Be merciful and slay me!

ALDERETE.

The truth! the truth! Where hidest thou the gold?
And I will end thy torment.

TACUBA, *to* FARFAN.

O, slay me;
Thou, sir, thy dagger; quick, stab me. O! O!

AÇALAN.

Where is thy leader? (*Calling.*) Cortés! Cortés!
    Cortés!

Exit AÇALAN.

TACUBA.

Speed! speed! (*Struggling.*) O, sluggard death!

GUATEMOZIN.

O, Tacuba,

Weak Tacuba, bathe I in waters cool?
Is not this rippled fire that laves my feet?
Have we not keener pangs than fleshly burns?
A wound so large it gaps a crater's lips,
Unhealing, stony, deep to bowels of fire;
A torment all absorbing, and so wide
No other pains can broaden; but they fall
Into the profound, as stars into the sun,
Consuméd utterly. Mexico—my mother!

> *Enter* CORTÉS, ISTRISUCHIL, *and others, followers
> of* ISTRISUCHIL.

CORTÉS.

Have they confessed?

ALDERETE.

They still are obdurate.

CORTÉS.

This will blot me.   Remove the fires.   O, fool !

ALDERETE.

Stay, sir; a little more and they confess.

CORTÉS.

Remove the fires, Sir Alderete.   Thou
Didst motion this in me to my dishonor;
I am all hot with shame and rage.

ALDERETE.

But, sir——

FARFAN, *to* ALDERETE.

Provoke him not, or, like the avalanche,
Men near with muffled mouths, and dread to speak,
For fear a whisper discompose the air,
And pulse a mountain with a breath to fall,
Hasty and blind his rage descends on thee.

The prisoners are released.

Re-enter AÇALAN *and the* QUEEN, *and with them
enter* OYOT, CULQUIL, *and other* AZTEC *nobles;
they run to and embrace and support* GUATE-
MOZIN *and* TACUBA.

ALDERETE.

But, sir, we had grave ground for what we did :
A member of the household of this king,
Blood of his blood, was our assurance that
We hunted no bad coppice for our game.

AÇALAN.

What meanest thou ?

CORTÉS.

Canst thou lay hands on him ?

ALDERETE.

He tarries at my quarters.

CORTÉS.

Hasten there ;
Bring him to me ; we'll put them face to face.

Exit ALDERETE.

CORTÉS.

Attend the prisoners with proper care ;
Bind up their feet, and medicine with cooling
Lotions their burns.   King Guatemozin, speak ;
Art thou much burned ?

GUATEMOZIN.

       Much burned? it matters not;
I am more burned in spirit than in body;
I yielded thee my crown, my life, my all;
And thou didst promise me security.
You said my faith was cruel; devil worship;
Thou camest here more to release our souls
From hell's embrace than win an empire: ay,
Thou gavest me thy priest to teach me better.
The story of thy God becoming man,
And suffering death to honor righteous law,
That justice might not lose at mercy's hands,
Or truth be self-destroyed; but all triuned
In equal glory, dwell in th' act of Him
Who made the law, that guilty men might hope,
With fuller faith and purer lives, for peace
With God, moved me: I was almost a Christian;
I thought if this be false, it is the sweetest,
Holiest, grandest lie that ever spake
On human lips. But is your faith divorced
From practice? Has it home within the ear,
And passage of the lips, a house of winds,
No shelter in the heart? Is it but words
To fool the simple with? It seemeth so.
What god have ye been worshipping to-day?

            Re-enter ALDERETE *with* TIZOC.

ALDERETE.

This is the man.

AÇALAN.

The Prince Tizoc!

GUATEMOZIN.

Tizoc!

CORTÉS.

Tizoc, didst thou lay charges on the king
And Tacuba that they had hidden gold,
Our lawful spoil?   Speak, or thy silence is
The coward-answer of a guilty man.

TIZOC, *hesitating.*

Not on the king, but Tacuba.

ALDERETE.

Speak, soldiers,
Ye were witnesses; was it not on the king?

SOLDIERS.

Ay, ay; he charged them both.

AÇALAN.

          See to what straits
The rancor of his hate has carried him:
He was the enemy of Tacuba;
To compass him in ruin, his king, who loved
And favored him, must suffer. (*To* CORTÉS.) O, thou
    fiend!
Justice for us and for thyself, a tool
Of this man's villainy!

CORTÉS.

         We were hoodwinked;
A petty captive's tool.to our disgrace.

ISTRISUCHIL, *to* CORTÉS.

Give him to me.

CORTÉS.

  To die?

ISTRISUCHIL.

         I promise it.

CORTÉS.

Away with him!

ISTRISUCHIL.

    Tizoc, thy scoffs and curses
Come home to thee. I thank thee for the thought.

(*To his followers.*) Take him to Tezcuco into the fields;
Summon my slaves; let them with bills and mattocks
Slay him there. 'Way!   ⸱

                              TIZOC *is led away.*

CORTÉS.

            Let not the pains we caused
Linger your hearts when fleshly wounds are cured:
Our sorrow's healing take, and be heart well.

GUATEMOZIN.

Thy penitence is good; but better right
Should always rule, for right is might in th' end,
E'en in its overthrow victorious;
For every wrong doth breed a snaky brood
That twine where flowery chaplets should have wound,
Wounding the brows that deemed them ornaments.
It was a little thing to break thy oath;
Who will revenge the friendless captive's wrong?
The wrong! The wrong! Behold the evil king;
He rules as doth a tempest; whence his strength?
From loyalty, a love to that most like
Which children bear to parents; yet so pure,
And strong, and deathless thing becomes a curse.
He makes his subjects evil, then a storm
Against a storm, and evil self-destroyed.

But right in splendor orbed shines on the calm,
As the unclouded sun when winds are laid.

AÇALAN.

He swoons! his poor, abuséd body breaks!
Help! Help! He is convulsed.

OYOT.

             Raise up! He stands
Upon his fire-burned feet.

          GUATEMOZIN *gazes as into space.*

GUATEMOZIN.

           These ceiléd walls,
Translucent as a filmy web, no more
Are barriers to my eyes. A city stands—
Here—O, my Mexico, where hast thou gone?
A city of great temples, throngéd streets;
A multitude with blood upon their hands,
Smearing the gold they clutch. War! endless wars!
Brothers with brothers waging hell on earth.
Ay, Mexico is revenged. O, victory!

      He falls back into their arms exhausted.

THE END.